"Tom Disch is the Devil! He says he's God, but he's not. Read this book against my warning, and at your peril. Every page you turn will send you deeper into the abyss. Tom Disch is America's own Mephistopheles!"

  – ALICE K. TURNER, AUTHOR OF *The History of Hell*

"The god Disch is brilliant, startling, playful, vengeful, poetic, and kind of scary. As gods go, we could do worse. The writer Disch is brilliant, startling, playful, vengeful, poetic, and kind of scary. As writers go, there is no one better."

  – KAREN JOY FOWLER, AUTHOR OF *The Jane Austin Book Club*

"Diversely gifted…entirely original…joyously versatile…a unique talent."

  – NEWSWEEK

"Of course, Tom has always been Jovial…but an actual divinity? Only now must I relinquish my birthright atheism, in recognition of the presence of a literary god. An obscure Vietnamese cult worshipped Victor Hugo, and I was tempted, but that was long ago, and they have passed from the scene."

  – NORMAN RUSH, AUTHOR OF *Mating* AND *Mortals*

"One of the most remarkably talented writers around."

  – WASHINGTON POST BOOK WORLD

"When it comes to Thomas Disch, label makers scratch their heads…. This literary chameleon redefined science fiction with novels that have been compared to the best from Orwell to Huxley, wrote bestselling children's books about talking kitchen appliances, earned censure from the Catholic Church for an off-Broadway play, published light verse, twisted the pulp conventions of gothic fiction, experimented with interactive software, and demolished the American poetry establishment, UFO cults, and other sacred cows in brilliant critical essays."

  – MINNEAPOLIS STAR-TRIBUNE

"Novelist, poet, and critic, he has become a most significant literary presence."

  – AMERICAN ACADEMY OF ARTS AND LETTERS

"I first came to believe in God when he successfully cured my cancer in 1969. A few years later he again answered my prayers by laying his hands on my first wife's belly and ensuring that our child would be a son. On almost every occasion when I have prayed sincerely and selfishly to God in whatever country I have been in he has answered me with his generous blessings most recently when he cured my diabetes in what I call the Miracle of the I-35 Dairy Queen. I cannot worship nor give my heart to a more beneficent or loving God than He. I have thanked God on every occasion I have been presented with a major literary prize or when those I consider my literary rivals and enemies have been denied awards or been struck with deadly diseases."

— MICHAEL MOORCOCK, AUTHOR OF *Stealer of Souls* AND *Behold the Man*

"A lovely, funny, interesting, incisive, and wonderfully blasphemous novel."

— JEFF VANDERMEER, AUTHOR OF *City of Saints and Madmen* AND *Shriek*

"It has been the happy fate of myself, my twin brother Greg, and our two younger sibs, Gary and Nancy, to have grown up with a god for an older brother. Sometimes it has been difficult to get along with such a perfect know-it-all, but didn't Jesus's siblings have the same blessed problem? What can I say? We adore him."

— JEFFREY JAMES DISCH

"I had never thought of Tom as stooping to God before, but it turns out to have been a good idea. It's good to hear from a Voice up there that knows the score, knows how to share His laughter with those who are mostly victims of His terrible laugh, knows that He too is art of the Joke. So please stay on high. Do us all Worlds of good."

— JOHN CLUTE

THE WORD OF GOD

Books by Thomas M. Disch

FICTION

The Genocides (1965)
Mankind Under the Leash (1966)
One Hundred and Two H-Bombs (1966)
Echo Round His Bones (1967)
Camp Concentration (1968)
Under Compulsion (1968)
The Prisoner (1969)
Getting Into Death and Other Stories (1973)
334 (1974)
The Early Science Fiction Stories of Thomas M. Disch (1977)
On Wings of Song (1979)
Fundamental Disch (1980)
Neighboring Lives [with Charles Naylor] (1981)
The Man Who Had No Idea (1982)
The Businessman: A Tale of Terror (1984)
The Brave Little Toaster (1986)
The Brave Little Toaster Goes to Mars (1988)
The M.D.: A Horror Story (1992)
The Priest: A Gothic Romance (1995)
The Word of God (2008)
The Wall of America [forthcoming] (Tachyon, 2008)

NON-FICTION

The Castle of Indolence: On Poetry, Poets, and Poetasters (1995)
The Dreams Our Stuff Is Made of: How Science Fiction Conquered the World (1998)
The Castle of Perseverance: Job Opportunities in Contemporary Poetry (2002)
On SF (2005)

THOMAS M. DISCH

THE WORD OF GOD

or, Holy Writ Rewritten

TACHYON PUBLICATIONS | SAN FRANCISCO

Cover design by Ann Monn
Interior design & composition by John D. Berry
The text and display typeface is Adobe Jenson Pro, designed by Robert Slimbach, with Herculanum, designed by Adrian Frutiger, on the title page

Tachyon Publications
1459 18th Street #139
San Francisco, CA 94107
(415) 285-5615
www.tachyonpublications.com

Series editor: Jacob Weisman

ISBN 13: 978-1-892391-77-3
ISBN 10: 1-892391-77-5

Special limited edition:
ISBN 978-1-892391-80-3

Printed in the United States of America
by Worzalla

First Edition: 2008

9 8 7 6 5 4 3 2 1

∽ to Ben Downing ∼

A Doll's Prayer

Now I lay me down to die
and bite my lip so's I won't cry.
If I should go to sleep instead
I pray I will not wet my bed.

— BETSY P

THE WORD OF GOD

Chapter One

LET THERE BE LIGHT.

There, the word is spoken and the universe has been brought into existence, and the Enlightenment along with it. We'll proceed from there. The important thing, always, is to have made a beginning. That's certainly been the way when I've written fiction, and Holy Writ probably works the same.

The title was no problem at all. It came in the proverbial flash. Whereas the subtitle has kept morphing ever since. Earlier versions have been variations on "And How You Can Be Too" or its opposite; then, off on another tangent, "Memoirs of an American Divinity." The latter, a tip of the hat to the transcendental tradition that covers such a broad range of Yankee divines as Emerson, Ann Lee, Joseph Smith, Mary Baker Eddy. Not all of them gods of an absolute and omniscient variety, like me, but prophets who've felt themselves to be on a par with Mohammed and whose scriptures have been accorded a similar reverence by large numbers of their fellow citizens. As polls keep showing, and media is ever reminding us, we Americans are a very religious nation, whose natural element is belief.

As to the revelations I mean to unfold, many will be of that traditional High Utterance that lays down laws and offers delectable previsions of heaven and saber-rattling fantasies of enemies horribly revenged, but there will also be talks of a friendlier locker-room character (the more American side of the vision), with homespun scriptures sometimes verging on whimsy. But nowhere will there be irreverence. Indeed, it's precisely in the more playful and paradoxical passages that seekers may find the touch-stones of a perfected faith, for faith is never more perfectly rooted in the soul than when one can truly believe in something one knows to be preposterous, like Noah's Ark. Christ had a special love for children and for simpletons (the poor in spirit); I can do no less.

Years ago, back before I knew myself to be divine, I lived next door to two Mormon missionaries in the Mexican town of Amec-ameca, an hour south of Mexico City. In all of Amecameca, they were the only other people who spoke English, and they delighted, in a true missionary spirit, in arguing about religion, and in partic-ular they liked to controvert Darwin and his theory of evolution. They had books filled with gorgeous views of the Grand Can-yon, which (it was maintained) had not been formed by the long drudgery hypothesized by secular humanist geology textbooks but assembled from raw materials in the time it takes to make an omelet. That this flew in the face of orthodox scientific wisdom was clearly a source of pleasure to my two neighbors.[1] Logical dif-ficulties only kindled their faith to a brighter glow and made their voices louder.

It is the special beauty of faith, that, like the fabled Phoenix, it draws its life from the flames that destroy it. It flies as it dies. A moth is the same in some ways, and it is the business of gods and of their prophets to light such beguiling flames that the faithful

---

1 Their names, I confess, I have forgotten. Even God nods.

cannot escape their supernal charm. The Jonestown suicides in Guyana, the Aum Shinrikyo cult's intended massacres, and militant Islam's achievements across the globe are all instances of the destructive power of faith. I'd like to assure my own faithful readers that I don't intend to lure them to any such immolation of themselves and others. If that makes me seem a lesser sort of a god, so be it. Like Christ, I shall defer slaughter and reprisals to the afterlife. Here and now, in the little time remaining, my enemies and competitor-gods will find that their threats and execrations will be powerless against the buckler and shield of my divine equanimity and sense of humor. All my justice shall be poetic.

The Greek gods were good at the same sort of thing, the way they'd find some fitting metamorphosis for anyone who pissed them off, turning house-proud Arachne into a spider and beautiful Io into a cow. But their cruelties and vendettas were not their defining features, nor yet their loves, wonderful as those were. Their beauty, then? Surely, that was a considerable asset, and any worshipper allowed inside one of their temples for a glimpse of Zeus or Apollo or Venus or Minerva must have been unnerved and overawed by their larger-than-life stature and command of good form. Gods then were expected to look terrific.

The Jews and their fellow monotheists had a less capital-intensive ideal: their god was just a voice in their heads — at least most of the time. Or words in a book. (Like the words in this book? you well might ask.) Their beauty did not need the high-priced skills of a Phidias, just a capable script-writer and a lector of sufficient charisma. It helps to have a naive audience, of course. Any parent can play Santa, and shamans don't need a college degree. The holy writings of Joseph Smith and L. Ron Hubbard will never qualify either prophet for inclusion in the Library of America. (And my own chances in that regard? They might seem slim, but only

God knows what may happen in the fullness of time — and I'm not telling!)

Literary merit doesn't matter much with Holy Writ. What matters is the faith that its faithful can bring to it. In dramas of faith the spotlight is always trained on the believer, on the born-again sinner being dunked in the baptismal pool or the martyr being thrown to the lions or the Palestinian child swaddled in the ammo-belts of his or her exemplary suicide. Their astonishing actions act to authenticate the gods they believe in. Doubt their gods and the believers' lives have been in vain. That's why it is good manners and simple prudence not to be express skepticism about the faith of strangers.

Again, I hasten to assure readers that I do not mean to solicit their self-immolation or even their total immersion in the pages ahead. I *do* have a program for the conduct of American foreign policy, and a few simple rites and superstitions I would have you observe, but I'll hold off on those things until we know each other better and I have been able to explain the tenets of our faith — and its commandments.

The first of which, like that of the Mosaic law, is that you stay seated where you are and continue reading *this* Holy Writ and have no other gods before you, nor any other author, for at this point in the drama of your conversion the two amount to the same thing. Not that there will be any terrible consequences if you put this Writ aside and enjoy some other licit pleasure for a while, for as I am not the kind of divinity that insists on corporal punishment now or in the hereafter, not even of such an indirect or non-miraculous kind as tornados or the arthritis I have to put up with. Life is hard enough in those regards without God adding to it.

Of course, doubters *will* experience an inner spiritual anguish of indescribable intensity as a result of being removed from my divine presence, but (here's another fine divine paradox) they won't know that they're in such a wretched state, just as the congenitally blind don't know what they're missing vis-à-vis vision.

Does all this begin to seem silly? It should. Pompous and grandiose? Absolutely. That has usually been my response to those zealots who have threatened me with fire, brimstone, and eternal punishment. I suspect them, as well, of ill-repressed sadistic tendencies, as though they would not be averse to administering some of their promised torments themselves, as agents of the latest holy inquisitions, if only they were not required elsewhere to sing in the heavenly choir.

So is this Holy Writ or isn't it? Am I being serious? Yes, and then some. What I propose to write about in these sacred pages is what the whole God-business looks like to someone who not only doesn't believe in God but who, moreover, doesn't believe in the belief of those most aggressively pious, most loudly devout. The only way effectively to convey my own sense of the matter is to arrogate to myself the same absolute authority, the same more-than-Papal infallibility, the same maddeningly smug chutzpah that True Believers of all varieties have armed themselves with: the Jesus freaks and Jehovah's Witnesses, the Tartuffes and Elmer Gantrys, the imams and ayatollahs, the redneck judges with two-ton Tablets of the Law they want to plunk down on the courthouse lawn and the archbishops campaigning against abortion, all the while they play three-card monte with their cadres of pedophile priests. To paraphrase a popular song, if they loved God half as much as they say they do, they wouldn't do all the things we can see them do.

Chapter Two

IT IS CHRISTMAS MORNING, 2004, even as I sit here at my keyboard typing "It is Christmas morning, 2004." The birthday of my competitor and a suitable occasion to speak of my own birth, back on February 2, 1940. As it happens I have already written a chapter or two on that theme (more of an Annunciation scene, in fact, but close enough), which was to be part of another, unfinished novel. I'm sure it's there somewhere on my hard drive, like a glacier that's been calved into the Antarctic Ocean. A god-like mistake, in its way, but a great frustration, even so.

So now I have to write a proper chapter on the theme of the Nativity and how it was celebrated on this darkest and most drear of holidays. At a national level it was a disaster, with whole busloads of people in Indiana trapped in their buses by blizzards, while on the other side of the International Date Line it may have been the worst catastrophe of all time thanks to the tsunami that devastated Sumatra, Thailand, Bangladesh, India, Sri Lanka, and some of the Somalian coast. Here at home Charlie's life has become one big tangle of prostheses, the most nightmarish of which is a vacuum pump that makes an erratic sucking sound (when it's not sounding its malfunction alarm), which it does both day and night. Even so, he is officially ambulatory, and so we have both been getting Christmas shopping done. After dinner last night (Chinese take-out supplemented with leftover roast pork, very tasty even if intended as a parody of the Disch Xmas-eve tradition of tuna fish chow mein) we unwrapped our presents: for Charlie, mostly clothes chosen to accommodate his new prostheses, although he did get a DVD of Bartoli singing two Haydn scenas, which we watched after the unwrapping; for me, some nice clothes as well, and a DVD of two Stravinsky ballets, plus three books, one of them precisely suited to citation in this chapter. If this were the cyber-utopia prophesied by the media, I would link you to the publisher's site where you could enjoy some of the book's 100+ color plates of paintings and sculptures of the Annunciation,[2] which is the book's one-word title.

It was just before bedtime, after we'd gorged on *bellissima* Bartoli, and while I was riffling through the centuries' variations of the theme of Madonna and Angel, it occurred to me that I had my own variation in cold storage, one that had yet to be born into print, and that expropriating that from *Tom's Divine Comedy* (which may never be finished) would be a better way to celebrate and cross-reference Christmas than what I'd earlier planned to do in Chapter 2.

Which was to do a riff on Dylan Thomas's opening line "Rage! rage against the dying of the light." A natural *sequela* to "Let there be light," and a springboard to a long litany of complaints concerning how my particular light seems to be dying. To wit, that I'm a few weeks shy of sixty-five and feeling the chill of death, the decrescendo of my career, and an across the board disillusionment with the culture around me. Indeed, that disillusionment was to have been the theme of a book-length rant I'd contracted to write for

---

2 *Annunciation* (Phaidon Press, 2000).

Harcourt Brace, *The Folly of Now: The Arts in the Age of Absurdity*, and then, just a month ago, uncontracted as the vultures of ill health, anxiety, and melancholy tore at my liver.

That's been the dark side of this winter solstice. But it's the job of any divinity to remind people of the bright side of things as well. The days will be getting longer. Just be patient. The most annoying of the prostheses will be removed, and Charlie will be able to travel farther away from Beth Israel and to feed the chickadees he dotes on and squeeze at least another lovely summer from Fate.

As for me and the dying of my light, this god is not about to die any time soon. Not this morning, as I write, nor tonight, after I've made our turkey dinner, not ever. Gods don't die, or if we do, we're resurrected before we've been forgotten. These days you don't even have to be a god to be resurrected. Faith will accomplish the same thing. Indeed, you needn't even die to be resurrected, if you can believe all those best-selling novels about the Rapture.

It's not just Christians who can expect a pleasant and everlasting afterlife. There are squadrons of suicide bombers, some within sight of today's tsunami, who've been promised a poolside of seventy virgins and all eternity to accomplish their defloration.

I hope that does not sound like scoffing. In today's multicultural multiculture scoffing is as verboten as swastikas or an inappropriate touch. We must all respect other people's faiths, no matter how ludicrous they may seem, and then they will respect ours.

Take Christmas, for instance, and its prequel, the Annunciation. In the diocesan museum of Cologne there is a lovely Annunciation of painted wood with a clay figure of Mary, the angel, God the Father, *and* the Holy Ghost hovering up by the rafters in the form of a white dove. An aviform Holy Ghost is a regular figure in most Annunciations, and often the clinching detail. Both Mary and God the Father are just ordinary people, like you and me, and any angel is a bit like Santa, hard to believe literally in after a certain age. But birds are real and everywhere and uncannily Other. You can bring them bread crumbs in the city park and, if you're patient, feed them from your hand. And though you might think you're brighter than those birds, just try and fly like them. In that not inconsiderable respect any pigeon is nearer to God than we.

And that is the first proof of my own Godhead. I have had a lot of experience flying. I've even written a novel on the subject,[3] and a short story, "How to Fly,"[4] which offers, within its brief compass, a good deal of practical advice to novice flyers. I will admit that as I've aged I've flown less often, but Jehovah is said to have rested after six days, and other gods have pooped out in their own ways. Wotan doesn't sing a note in the final *Ring* opera. The important thing is that, like the Holy Ghost, I *used* to fly a great deal.

Howsoever, there are more cogent reasons than his knack for flight as to why the Holy Ghost has been my favorite person of the Holy Trinity. He is the god of Pentecost, who descended in the form of fire to kindle a kindred fire of faith in the hearts of the apostles. Before Pentecost they were all cowering out of sight in an attic, afraid they'd meet the same terrible fate as Jesus. But after they'd been zapped by the Holy Ghost they were hyped, ready for martyrdoms of their own. That's what Faith can do for you. It helps you die with a smile on your face, in the embrace of my eternal love. So forget Dylan Thomas. There's no need to rage, because the light is not dying. It's there in the stars above, and in every light bulb on every Christmas tree in every living room in the whole country. And it's also there in the haloes of Mary and the Archangel beside her and, even more brightly, in the nimbus around

3   *On Wings of Song* (St. Martin's Press, 1979).
4   *The Man Who Had No Idea* (Gollancz, 1982).

the Holy Ghost, though as a matter of fact the Holy Ghost in the Cologne museum is missing a nimbus, since he's a three-dimensional clay figure there, and those were the days before electric light bulbs. But the Holy Ghost on the cover of the book, who is shown suspended over Mary's rumpled bed, has a splendid nimbus, gold at the core and blue around the edges, not unlike my own, on the right day, in a room with subdued lighting.

Why, you may have wondered, am I telling you all this? Shouldn't a god show more discretion? Christ, after all, always pussyfooted about the question of whether he was Elisha or Elijah, the Messiah or the Son of God. He left it to his disciples and to posterity to make those claims on his behalf. I expect much the same thing will be the case with respect to the final acknowledgment of my divinity (and the merits of my poetry, as well).

That being said, there are ways in which Christ's reticence in this matter makes one wonder whether *he* was quite confident as to his Godhead. Greek gods, like Zeus and Apollo, might tomcat about disguised as ordinary mortals (and I've done the same), but sometimes with Jesus it doesn't seem like a disguise. If it weren't for all the miracles, from that star in the East down to his glorious resurrection, you might think he was just another prisoner on Death Row long, long ago.

Well, that was then, and this is now. I am not a jealous god myself, and anyone who wants to believe in Jesus and adore him and turn their other cheek, etc., is welcome to do so under my covenant.

And with respect to my friendly feelings toward Jesus, I just remembered there's a story I wrote about him during the brouhaha last spring about Mel Gibson's *Passion of the Christ*. So without more preamble, let me present, as a coda to this chapter, not a Christmas story but one on the darker theme of the crucifixion.

The Second Coming of the Christ

The Handel Festival had been going on for four hundred years. Jesus had attended more *Messiah*s by this point than had ever been performed in the entire history of mortal man. Eternity can be like that, which in some ways can be a good thing. When one's favorite dessert recurs eternally, it's easier to resist temptation. Jesus loved crème brûlée, but even with crème brûlée enough isn't just enough, it can get to be too much. So he *could* just walk out of heaven's infinite auditorium if he chose to. Only he didn't. He was still enjoying his dessert, metaphorically speaking.

In any event, the resurrected choir of the Fort Lauderdale Civic Chorus together with musicians from the Holbein Consort had just performed an encore of "For Unto Us a Child Is Born," when St. Peter barged into the Holy Trinity's box, with his usual air of anxious self-importance, to announce: "Lord! Lord, you'll never believe this. There's a celestial anomaly happening at this very moment. You can return to Earth! But you've got to be quick."

Jesus took a look at Furtwängler taking another bow there at the podium and the heavenly host applauding him, and then winked at St. Peter. "What the hell, let's do it. No one will miss me, and the festival's scheduled to go on for a few more centuries. We can be back before it's over."

Peter was pleased to have been included in Jesus's plans without his having had to ask. He'd enjoyed his life on Earth, and his job overseeing admissions at Heaven's gate kept terrestrial matters always right under his nose, fresh as a breeze off the Sea of Galilee. "Let's," Peter agreed. "Yes, let's."

They walked over to the very brink of heaven and peered down at a dark illimitable ocean, which was without bound and without dimension, where eldest Night and Chaos held eternal anarchy amidst the noise of endless wars.

"Oh my," said Jesus, "I'd forgotten what a long way off it is."

Peter nodded agreement. If he squinted hard he could see Iraq, with its engines of war still roaring and smoking, and nearby the holy city of Jerusalem, so altered since he and Jesus had last been there. In the building next to where they'd had the Last Supper was a kosher pizzeria, and parked outside of it a busload of American tourists from Macon, Georgia. They were eating their pizza slices with four-cheese topping inside the bus because it was cooler there.

But that was not where the celestial anomaly would be letting them off.

"There," said Jesus, without raising his voice. (When you're omniscient you don't have to insist overmuch.) He pointed to the middle of the big green area that was North America. "That's where we're headed."

As soon as it was pointed out to him, Peter knew that Jesus was right. And the moment he *knew* that, the celestial anomaly kicked in and they were there. Faith works like that, and nobody has ever had a stronger faith than Peter. It was the main reason he'd been chosen to head up the apostles.

In all essential ways Kansas City was much like Jerusalem or Rome. Lots of people milling about, none of them aware of each other except for a few predators on the sidelines waiting for an opportunity to score. Marks of weakness, marks of woe. Hunger for all kinds of different things. Peter had forgotten that feeling. He had a sudden intense craving for eel, its special chewiness, the way even the bones seemed slippery when you tried to chomp down on them. The world of the flesh! It all started to come back.

Jesus walked over to a shop window to admire a recliner upholstered in Brazilian leather in a shade of burgundy. The interior of the store was filled with other pieces of furniture, the luxuries all crammed together like passengers on a pleasure barge. Heaven seemed drab in comparison. And the carpentry seemed of the best quality. If there was time, Jesus hoped they might visit the workshop where these goods had been made.

"Oh dear," said Peter. "Oh my." As his ruddy cheeks grew redder, he tried to steer Jesus away from the shop window so that he might not see the mirror within — and in that mirror themselves, in the flesh they'd borrowed for this occasion.

Too late. Jesus, though not exactly a mind reader, was quick to pick up what other people were thinking. He saw his image in the mirror — and burst out laughing.

"Goodness!" said Peter. "I have to apologize. It never occurred to me that when we came here we wouldn't be…ourselves."

Jesus fingered the cuff of his sweater, then lifted his hand to sniff the wool. Oddly, it had no smell.

"It's strange," said Peter, "but when I look directly at you, I see the Jesus I know. It's only in the mirror you look like…someone else."

"What's the old saying? 'O what a gift the Giftie gie us, to see ourselves as others see us.' That's what's mirrors are for, I suppose — so we can see the selves that other people see. But it is a convenience, really that when we come here we should look like the folks about us. If we looked as we did in Galilee, we'd come off as a very odd couple."

"I suppose you're right. Only this does seem…less than dignified."

"Oh, I was never one to stand on my dignity," said Jesus.

Peter had his own ideas about that, but he bit his tongue. He knew better than to contradict the Lord God Almighty. The meek, he reminded himself, are blessed. That, however, was a part of Jesus's program that Peter had always had trouble with. The meek may well be blessed, but they didn't seem to have inherited the earth at this point in the twenty-first century. In any case, Jesus had never seemed particularly meek to Peter, not by any definition of meek he'd ever heard.

Someone in a blue cap tried to press a piece of paper into Peter's hand. Peter edged away.

"Discount tickets," the man insisted. "Check it out."

By the miracle so long ago of Pentecost, Peter could understand any language, even in its written form. In his own language, Aramaic, Peter had never learned to read. Those were simpler times back then, and literacy was limited to scribes and tax accountants. Fishermen had no need for ABCs.

But Peter could read the flyer he'd been handed, which was an advertisement for Mel Gibson's hit movie, *The Passion of the Christ*, which had already earned box office receipts, according to the flyer, of over half a billion dollars. There was a picture of the Christ in the movie (not an especially good likeness) and a coupon that you could redeem at the Loews box office for two dollars off on any adult ticket purchased for a weekday matinee.

"Are you saved?" the man in the blue cap inquired. "Do you recognize Christ as your Redeemer?"

"Oh, definitely," Peter said, trying to keep a straight face. Wouldn't this fellow have been amazed if he knew that he was in the Redeemer's presence at this very moment?

"Have you been baptized?" the man insisted earnestly.

Peter wanted to say that he'd been baptized in the River Jordan, but he reminded himself that it's the meek who inherit the earth. So he just nodded.

The man seemed suspicious in some way. "You're not Jewish, are you?"

He was, of course. They both were, but he didn't see how that was any concern of this fellow. He and Paul had hashed it all out long ago that Jews and Gentiles were all the same in the eyes of the Lord. Should he explain it again to this guy?

"We have been circumsised," said Peter in an equable tone, "in the flesh *and* in the spirit, but we have also received a new life through the baptism of Our Savior's blood. Does that answer your question?"

The man nodded uncertainly.

"Tell us," said Jesus, sensing the man's discomfort, "about this movie. Have you seen it yourself?"

"Not yet. Our whole church is going as a group on Sunday. I'm doing this now to help pay for our block of tickets."

"Sunday is your Sabbath here, isn't it?" Peter said, in the gently prosecutorial tone he used when sinners came to Heaven's gate.

"It's the Sabbath just about everywhere. Isn't it?"

"No," said Jesus, gently. "But I think what my friend is intimating is: if Sunday's the Sabbath, and a day of rest, how can you be attending a movie?"

"It's not just any movie!" the man protested. "It's the Passion! It's like going to church a second time."

"It doesn't really come in the category of helping an ox out of a pit," Peter huffed.

"And what day is today?" Jesus asked, shielding his eyes from the glare of the sun as it slotted into the groove formed by the huge buildings on either side of the street.

"It's Friday," the man answered. "Why? Is that a problem?"

"In terms of using this discount coupon," said Jesus, "I'm afraid it is. Sabbath for *us* begins at sunset. Which is just moments away.

Will it still be valid tomorrow?"

"No, that'd be Sunday. This is only for weekday matinees."

"Well, then, on Monday, we will try to see your movie. Thank you for the coupon." Peter folded it up and put it into his fanny pack. Then with Jesus he walked west through the amazing canyon of Osage Street, among Kansas City's multitudes, toward the sun.

There were so many wonderful things to do in Kansas City that some time went by taking in the sights and schmoozing with publicans and sinners before Peter remembered the coupon in his fanny pack. When he did come upon it, as he was foraging for the card that opened the door to their hotel room, he felt a twinge of conscience. The fact was that he didn't really want to see the movie at the Loews multiplex. The crucifixion had been an awful experience for everyone involved, and Peter did not think Jesus would want to be reminded of it.

Among the people they'd met in the bars and parks and gardens of the city, many had already been to the movie, and they were almost evenly divided between those who felt that the depiction of Jesus's ordeal was accurate (and therefore edifying) and those who felt Mel Gibson had gone too far. The latter were concerned less for the movie's accuracy than for its effect on children.

All these movie-related conversations had been conducted by Peter while Jesus was engaged with other Kansas Citians trading jokes and parables, for which he seemed to have a limitless appetite. His favorite new parable so far concerned a pair of drinking companions in an Irish bar. In a series of inquiries, back and forth, they determined that they were both from the same small town in County Kerry, had both attended the same school, and even graduated in the same year! At the moment they discover this, the phone rings, the bartender answers and says, to his caller,

"Oh, there's nothing much happening here. The O'Reilly twins came in, both completely drunk." It was a funny parable illustrating the fallibility of human memory, but Jesus really could not manage a credible Irish brogue. Even in Aramaic he'd never been able to handle accents.

What most tempted the two of them to use the coupon was sheer homesickness, the chance to hear Aramaic spoken again. But at the cost of reliving the crucifixion? Of course there had been occasions in Eternity when the same subject had come up. Bach had his Passions, Grünewald and Rubens their Crucifixions, and there were various versions of the Seven Last Words, but the movies on the subject had generally tempered accuracy with an averted gaze. Peter had been crucified himself, upside-down, but when *Quo Vadis* had come out, with Finlay Currie playing the role, Peter hadn't had the stomach to watch that scene. Indeed, anything that brought back his days in Rome made him queasy. It didn't even have to be about the martyrdom of the Christians. *Spartacus* had been a nightmare. Slaves crucified as far as the eye could see. No wonder Rome's civilization had self-destructed. Human nature wasn't designed to be so unremittingly cruel. Or maybe it was. Terrible things had happened all through human history. The Huns, the Nazis, Armenia, Rwanda, the list went on. Jesus liked to think (and so did Peter) that his crucifixion had somehow settled the score once and for all, but there were times when it didn't seem that simple.

For those times the solution was Faith — and an averted gaze. But what happened when you were asked to bear witness? Indeed, at the actual crucifixion, back when, that had been exactly the job that Peter had funked. He'd fallen asleep in the olive garden, when he should have been standing guard, and then after Jesus had been arrested he'd denied that he even knew him on three separate occasions. Undoubtedly he would have his nose rubbed in that all over again in this damned movie.

So, on Monday, when they first might have caught a matinee performance at the multiplex, they'd decided instead to go to the Kansas City Zoo. They'd seen a tired old lion, and three mangy camels (their smell was a whiff of old times), and then an entire small herd of American buffalo, which neither of them had ever seen before except in movies. They'd had hot dogs for lunch, and ice cream cones. After all this time of being a disembodied spirit, the ice cream was, in a paradoxical way, very Heaven. The pork in the hot dog was another matter, though with all the spices and extender, the hot dog was not intensely unkosher. Nothing like the pork sausages outside the Coliseum. Even Jesus, who was used to his fleshly body, not having had to wait for the general resurrection like everyone else, seemed to have enjoyed their lunch at the zoo with unusual zest. Maybe it was having seen the way the old lion had torn into his bucket of whatever it was. The pleasures of the flesh!

That night back in their hotel room they'd watch a TV program called *Joan of Arcadia*, about an American virgin who is regularly visited by God, who assumes a human form in his visitation. These theophanies were more on the Greek or Roman model, always taking a different and usually rather droll form — a fat, dowdy old lady or a smart-alecky brat or a cop. And the import of the divine encounter was always a little ambiguous, leaving poor Joan hungry for some clarification. But Jesus found the program entertaining and even performed a little miracle so that when it was over they were able to speed-view the entire series to date in the twinkling of an eye. Sometimes there were advantages in being pals with the Almighty. Of course, the series eventually grew predictable and a little stale, but that was the way with most mortal endeavors, esthetic or otherwise. Freshness fades, and brightness falls.

The next day the coupon was still there in Peter's fanny pack, so after lunching on a plastic container of fruit salad from a deli near the hotel they went to the cineplex, redeemed the coupon, and found a pair of seats at a comfortable distance back from the screen. In deference to the movie's sacred theme there were no previews. The lights dimmed and there was a big R on the screen to indicate the violent character of the movie and then the moon appeared, and then the actor playing Jesus dripping with sweat from dread of what he knew was coming.

So was the real Jesus sitting beside Peter, though not quite to the same degree. The Jesus on the screen bore a better resemblance to the Christ of Galilee than the flesh Jesus had borrowed for this visit, and by the time the movie's Jesus had stomped on the head of the snake accompanying Satan, Peter's belief was totally suspended. He was back at Gethsemene, sword in hand, hacking an ear off the high priest's servant.

Jesus restored the ear to the man's head, but no one paid the least attention. They bound him up in a length of chain and started dragging him into the city, but not before knocking him over the side of a cliff. Neither Jesus nor Peter had been ready for that. They gasped in shock. The chain kept Jesus from plummeting to his death, and he was hauled up to the road again, but at that point Jesus stopped looking at the screen except in furtive glances. At the moment Jesus was brought before Caiaphas, Jesus excused himself to go to the men's room, and so he missed the next terrible thing that happened — when Caiaphas struck Jesus in the face with his ivory-tipped staff. That was another detail, like the fall from the cliff, that Mel Gibson had just invented, and though there was nothing wrong with that exactly, it did serve to remind Peter that this was not a documentary but an imaginative re-creation. He wasn't really obliged to stick with it to the end. But just as he was stirring himself to join Jesus in the men's room, Jesus returned to his seat (annoying the people who'd had to stand up again to let him get by).

They watched the rest of the *Passion* all the way to the rolling of the credits. Peter was thankful for the respite and the chance to think of something besides the horrors of the crucifixion. The way the crow had pecked out the eyes of the bad thief. Awful. The spray of blood after the lance's *coup de grâce*. As to the resurrection, it was there, but in such a half-hearted, pro forma way it didn't register as any kind of counterweight or redemption.

So they were grateful for the credits. It was, as usual, humbling to be reminded of what an army of technicians it takes to make a movie. And to be reminded, furthermore, that the movie had been, as much as Grünewald's gruesome crucifixion, an artifice.

"At a certain point," Jesus said later, at the hotel's coffee shop, "I just blanked out. I couldn't empathize, even with my own sufferings. Up to a certain point, yes, I was there, it was all happening. But then..." He shook his head. "I actually was more upset in the scenes with Judas. What a good actor."

"Yes, wasn't he," said Peter, stirring more sugar into his coffee. "And those children tormenting him, little demons, quite upsetting. It was like a miniature version of your story. Very odd."

"It made me feel sorry for him."

Peter looked askance. "Now, Lord, you can't say *he* didn't know what he was doing. You're not going to forgive him at the last judgment, are you?"

Jesus laughed. "No, of course not. Though I think Mel Gibson might. Do you know, I'm so glad that's over with."

"The movie?" Peter asked.

"Oh, not just the movie," said Jesus. "The flesh. The world."

"I know," said Peter with a sigh. "I have to deal with it every day. The people at the gate, all the arguments. The excuses: 'I never really meant to hurt them.'"

"But look at the bright side," said Jesus.

"The lilies of the field?" Peter asked teasingly. That was an old bone of contention between them. Peter didn't think the Lord gave proper credit to all the toiling and spinning that gets things done in the workaday world.

"Surely they're one part of the bright side," said Jesus. "Ah well. What do you say we head back to heaven tonight?"

Chapter Three

THERE NOW, would you say that was blasphemous? I think it's at least as reverent as Mel Gibson's movie, and surely more meek and mild in its overall tone. But such was not the view of the editors who read it, who were unanimous in advising me that while it might be charming, some of their readers would be outraged by its cavalier way of dealing with a divinity. They didn't realize, of course, that as a divinity myself I was entirely within my rights to speak of other gods in a familiar or jesting way. Even now that I have manifested myself to all the nations, there will still be editors whose doubts will override their literary judgment. That's assuming they had been candid in the first place and hadn't rejected the story, as they'd rejected so many others earlier, for the simple reason that they hate my guts.

Anyhow, enough of Jesus. He's had his holiday, and today is the day *after* Christmas, and my Writ has scarcely got beyond the prolegomenon stage. Indeed, it's actually the day after the day after Christmas, the rest of yesterday having been frittered away in hunting down and boning up on my tattered copy of *Tristram Shandy*. I thought Sterne's novel might supply just the fuel I needed to write an account of my own conception and birth, but once again Sterne's unrelenting whimsies, curlicues, and digressions defeated my good intentions, and I fear that *Tristram Shandy* will join *Don Quixote* as one of the masterpieces of world literature that I can never be credited with having read. (I still have hopes for *The Tale of Genji*, but I don't see how that could be grist for my mill at this juncture.)

However, fate has smiled, and in the course of looking for my thesaurus (which isn't here in the city), I came upon the grist I was looking for, a framed reproduction of a color print of Crespi's altarpiece, now at the National Gallery in Washington, of St. Mary of Egypt, in the arms of an angel, receiving Holy Communion for the last time. There is a second angel kneeling before her who holds a guttering torch. I've never seen the painting itself, since the uptown gallery that had scheduled it for exhibition canceled the show as soon as the painting was sold. But it was love at first sight with the print. Mary is in such a swoon. It is as though the host approaching her lips were the ultimate ravishing *crème brûlée*, eternity's best dessert. Keats's nightingale would probably be the musical equivalent, or Wagner's *Tristan und Isolde* (which we saw on Channel 13 last night, in a pared-down orchestral version).

A happy death, or death by happiness. Now more ever seems it rich to die, and all that jazz. Part of the problem with suicide is that there seems no way to guarantee that one's own passage to the other side will be so exquisitely catered as it is in Crespi's or Keats's or Wagner's versions. I tried suicide just the once, when I was eighteen, living in a sublet on West 16th, for no reason that I can remember. But what teenager, gay, penniless, and without friends, needs reasons? Anyhow it was a sincere attempt: I shut the windows, stuffed a towel under the door out to the hall, turned on the gas burners on the stove, and went to bed. When I awoke a few hours later, I was astonished that I wasn't dead, and after I'd opened the windows and returned the towel to the towel rack, I called Con Ed to complain. The man I talked to explained that Con Ed had long ago introduced an element into the gas that would make people nauseous before they could die, and that's why one no longer reads of suicides discovered in their ovens.

Though I pretended to be pissed off, I was secretly rather glad to have been foiled in my attempt, for it occurred to me that there were all sorts of things I might enjoy doing that I hadn't yet done. The first on the list was scuba diving at the Great Barrier Reef, something I still haven't got round to (though I've made three trips to Bermuda, where at least I got to dip my toe in the water). Whenever I talk to young people who so much as hint that their lives are taking them nowhere, etc., I ask if they have ever been to the Great Barrier Reef and then tell my edifying tale.

I doubt that what with my arthritis, my diabetes, and my disposition to pinch pennies, I will ever get to the Great Barrier Reef myself, any more than I will finish *Tristram Shandy* or *Don Quixote*, but Crespi's Mary is a good reminder of other incentives for hanging on, art chief among them. Last night's program of Levine conducting the Berlin Philharmonic in two hours of highlights from Wagner and Strauss was scarcely a rapture of four-star quality, but it had its *crème brûlée* moments.

And only now has it occurred to me that if I *had* been scuba diving at the Great Barrier Reef on Christmas Day I might have been one of 35,000 victims of that tsunami!

God works in mysterious ways, though perhaps I should not be the one to say so. Did I mention that in my rummaging about I discovered not only the Crespi print but also a diskette that had the cantos and intercantos of *Tom's Divine Comedy* in individual files? I did, so now I can take one giant step forward in this story by appending...

A Man of Mystery

The old gentleman in Room 334 came down to the lobby and took his seat in the alcove every afternoon at a quarter to six, just when most people were heading home from work. Sometimes his lady-friend was with him, sometimes the good-looking guy, sometimes both of them. He would open up his leather valise, a classy item with a single gold M stamped on it beneath the handle, take out a little sheaf of papers, and read aloud to his ladyfriend or the guy, who would listen very intently, eyes squinted half-shut, smoking Camels. The Leamington didn't ordinarily like women smoking in the lobby, and Helen would not have had the nerve to light up a cigarette when she came in, but then she wasn't a guest at the hotel. In fact, it wasn't all that long ago that she'd worked here, in the summer of '38, cleaning the rooms and making beds, but that was in the mornings, behind the scenes, and she didn't think any of the afternoon crew at the desk recognized her from back then. Wayne, in the bar connected to the hotel, was a friend from back then, and times such as now when the manager wasn't around he would let her take a free spritz of Coke into the lobby, a privilege usually reserved for hotel guests and their friends. It was nice of him, but even so, it made her feel uneasy. She had to watch her step if she didn't want to be asked to leave. There weren't that many hotels in downtown Minneapolis with comfortable lobbies where you could sit and read.

She always tried to dress as well as she could, her makeup careful, a veil across her face, and sheer nylons. Looking like she belonged in the Leamington was easier now in the warmer weather, as long as it didn't rain. Her winter coat was getting shabby, there was no concealing that, and the only umbrella available to her was a big, black men's umbrella with one rib broken, so on rainy days she just stayed at home in the upstairs bedroom of her father-in-law's house and listened to the radio or read *Collier's*. It was not a magazine she would have read by her own choice, but it came in the mail as part of Red's job. In any case when she came to the Leamington there was usually a movie magazine or the *Star* lying around somewhere in the lobby. Lacking that, she would get out the book that Father Windakiewiczowa had told her that she had to read. It was spread across her lap now, *A Series of Lectures on Social Justice*, and it was just as dull as that sounded. The priest who wrote it had his own radio program that was broadcast every Sunday evening, and Father Windakiewiczowa wanted her to listen to that, too, but enough is enough, and anyhow Red said the radio priest was a Nazi. Her father-in-law, on the other hand, seemed to think the Coughlin guy was God, or a close neighbor.

Even though his family was from Germany, or the German part of Switzerland, Red didn't like the Nazis. But then he was so old he'd fought against them in the war, though maybe fought was the wrong word since he'd been in the Navy and never once fired a gun. She figured most of his talk against the Nazis was a way of showing people he didn't like Germans, now that it looked like we might be going to war with them again. For her part Helen respected the old rule not to talk about politics or religion. Men didn't listen to you anyhow, even if you did try to put in your own two cents. Their eyes would just glaze over, as though a commercial had come on the radio in the middle of a ballgame. Like the old gentleman right now. His ladyfriend was going on a mile a minute — in what Helen guessed must be German, though the only German she knew was *Gesundheit!* — and he wasn't taking in a word. (In fact he was looking at *her* and pretending not to.)

She hadn't considered it before, but maybe the old gentleman was not only German but a genuine Nazi besides. He did have a mustache, though not a mustache like Hitler's, more like Clark Gable's in *Gone with the Wind* or *It Happened One Night*, her two favorite movies of all time. Her own father had had a mustache, the big old-fashioned kind, though she'd only ever seen him that way in the wedding picture, before he'd got so fat. That was the nice thing about the gentleman in the alcove, how skinny he was, despite his age. If *he* were on top of you having sex, you almost wouldn't notice it. Not that she'd ever given a thought to such a possibility, but you could always tell, with older man like that, what they were thinking about when they were thinking about sex. Without his ever saying a word, just by the way he looked at her from across the lobby, when he thought she couldn't see him.

Such as now. His ladyfriend was having another Camel (she was a real chain smoker), and this time, after he'd offered her a light, he opened up his own silver case and took out a cigarette and fit it into his little black holder. Helen didn't approve of men using cigarette holders, though she made exceptions for the President and for foreigners. Anyone, that is, who would have seemed more at home on a movie screen than out on the street.

Now there was no doubt about it: he was giving her the eye, and Helen, so as not to seem to be flirting, picked up her copy of Father Coughlin's book. Nothing could have been more dull and respectable, with its cover the color of dried mud. And the same taste, too, if books could be tasted, mud. She started in where she'd left off, on page 82: "When our armies meet on the field of battle, DuPont powder will send shot and shell screaming into their ranks... When the new gases developed in laboratories of the United States pour forth death and destruction — even our own civilian population, our women and children will be killed by the self-same gases. Who will win the next war — communist or capitalist, it matters not. The Du Ponts will be the real winners."[5]

The Du Ponts, Father Windakiewiczowa had explained, were Jews, or possibly not, but they represented the Jewish interests that were in control of international banking and had caused the Depression. Father Windakiewiczowa was always going on about the Jews, and the danger they posed to America, and how they were the same as Communists by another name. Red said that was all a lot of baloney and not to pay attention but he wanted her to keep taking instructions anyhow, for his parents' sake. All the Disches seemed to share Father Windakiewiczowa's opinion of Lutherans as being the next thing to Jews. It was a good thing they didn't know what Lutherans thought of *them*, with the nuns' babies buried in the basements of their convents and the priests no better than Count Dracula.

You had to wonder where people got their ideas. Imagine Father Windakiewiczowa getting anyone pregnant! The man had no more use for sex than a neutered cat. His only interest in sex, so far as Helen could tell, was to make certain she and Red weren't practicing birth control.

They were, of course, or they would have had more than the one accident, but she had enough common sense not to say so, even in confession, where you were supposed to produce your whole laundry list. Red, who'd been a Catholic his whole life and from a really pious family, said that it was enough in the confessional to say you'd committed a sin of impurity, and for how many times, and if the priest insisted on knowing more, then say it was a mortal sin and you'd never do it again, and most priests probably wouldn't hound you any further. Of course, the sin she'd been talking about with Red was her abortion, not the birth control,

---

5 *A Series of Lectures on Social Justice*, by Rev. Charles E, Coughlin (The Radio League of the Little Flower, 1935).

which Red said wasn't her sin anyhow, but his, since he was the one with the rubber.

Catholics were all lawyers. That was the fascinating thing about taking instructions, all the little ways you could cheat if you were a Catholic and it didn't count toward sending you to hell. With Lutherans it was like the whole world was doomed to hell, except at Christmas, or when the minister was in a good mood. And of course *all* the Catholics got sent there, just the way for Father Windakiewiczowa all Lutherans were sent there. She'd asked him what she would have to do to keep her family — and there were a lot of Gilbertsons — from going to hell, and his advice was to pray that they would be converted. Right!

Now the old gentleman's ladyfriend was getting up, at a signal from the good-looking younger guy, who was standing at the main entrance with a dripping umbrella. At the sight of the umbrella, Helen did a dismayed double take, because the weather forecast at noon hadn't said a thing about rain. Only an hour ago, when she'd come into the lobby, there wasn't more than a mist of clouds in the sky. And even now you couldn't *hear* a single raindrop. It was the kind of rain that just condensed around you. But she would be soaked before she got to the bus, never mind the time she would probably have to spend waiting.

A taxi was out of the question, even if she could have afforded one. There was almost nothing, in fact, that she could afford. She knew what she had in her purse — $1.85 — and that would have to last until Red came back with his road crew on Friday night. It was enough for her bus fare, a couple packs of Chesterfields, two shots at some other bar than the Leamington, and maybe a hamburger. Most of her meals she took with her in-laws, or else raided the icebox. There was always plenty there (unlike the Gilbertson pantry), because Red's father owned the corner grocery right across the street.

Well, let the weather do what it liked, it wasn't the end of the world. It just meant she'd have to be patient and sit out the rain. She had Father Coughlin to help her do that. She tried again — this time a speech called "The Menace of the World Court." Apparently there had been a danger, some years back, that America was surrendering its independence to the League of Nations. "America," the priest lamented, "instead of rescuing from the hands of international bankers the right to coin and regulate the value of money, instead of limiting the accumulation of wealth by the favored few... America is ready to join hands with the Rothschilds and Lazare Frères, with the Warburgs and the Morgans and the Kuhn-Loebs to keep the world safe for the inevitable slaughter."[6]

What was that all about? Was there really going to be another war even worse than the last one? And all because of bankers in New York? Father Coughlin seemed sure of it, and Father Windakiewiczowa likewise, but Helen didn't see how, even if there was a war, it would affect her. Red was over forty, so they weren't about to draft him, though that didn't stop him worrying about it. Her brothers would get drafted, but Russ and Maurie were already talking about the army as though it would be a good thing. The reason wars happened was probably so people like Russ and Maurie could wear uniforms and fire guns at each other like kids playing cops and robbers. At least that's what her friend Rhoda said, and Rhoda was probably the smartest person she knew. Not that it did her any good: she was always landing good jobs and then getting fired cause she'd wised off. There was a poem by Unknown in the book Rhoda had given her for Christmas that was very relevant on that score. Helen had memorized it so she could share it with Rhoda the next time they got together:

---

6 Ibid. p. 125.

> *A wise old owl lived in an oak;*
> *The more he saw the less he spoke;*
> *The less he spoke the more he heard:*
> *Why can't we all be like that bird.* [7]

Helen was running through the lines of the poem again (that was how poems *stayed* memorized), with her eyes closed to help her to concentrate, when Wayne from the bar came up beside her and said, "Hey, Sleeping Beauty."

"I am not sleeping," Helen protested indignantly, at the same time sitting up straighter in the overstuffed chair.

"Glad to hear it," said Wayne. "Wouldn't want to see you thrown out on the street when it's raining this way. Anyhow, I brought you this drink. Compliments of the old geezer over in the corner."

Helen looked with astonishment at the drink on the tray — it must have been a Manhattan cocktail, it had a cherry under its ice cubes — and then at the old gentleman, who had another kind of drink that he was holding up in her direction, as though to say *skoal*. Helen smiled the most tentative of smiles and wondered whether she should accept the drink on Wayne's tray. Her mouth was already watering at the thought of the cherry. She only hesitated from a concern for what the hotel would think.

On that score she was ready to trust Wayne's judgment. "Would it be okay?" she asked in a whisper. "I wouldn't want anyone to get the wrong idea."

"So far as the hotel goes there'd be no problem. It's cash in the till. I figure he wants someone to talk to, and you by preference to me."

---

7 "A Wise Old Owl," in *The Best Loved Poems of the American People*, selected by Hazel Felleman. (Doubleday, 1936)

"Then I will," she decided. She took the Manhattan and held it up, smiling her thanks.

The man lifted his chin in acknowledgment, just the way her father-in-law would have. Then with his free hand he patted the cushion on the couch beside him, where his ladyfriend had been sitting.

The girl seemed as shy as a goldfinch in a cage, but just as with a caged bird, flight being impossible, what could she do but ruffle her pretty feathers and shift sideways on her perch? In point of fact she was more sparrow than goldfinch, her plumage being distinctly proletarian, the shoes particularly woeful (as Erika had pointed out, when they'd been anatomizing the poor creature). But for pathos nothing, not even Chaplin's bowler, could excel the wisp of a veil wrapped around her toque of faux loden with its single, sad, aspiring feather. And ah! the rubious lips, the crimson nails, the squared-off shoulders of the dowdy dress. It was an apparition of the purest celluloid: not the native product, however, not Pickford or Gish, nor yet an exotic import like the incomparable Garbo (though there was, to do her justice, a touch of Garbo in the cheekbones, the thrust of the jaw), but an American facsimile, patently inauthentic, a kind of nursery masquerade of grownup fashion, rustic and irresistibly charming.

He tipped his chin a little higher and called across the lobby (there was no one to overhear, only he and the girl and the attendant from the bar): "Won't you join me? Please," marveling all the while at his own boldness; which here in America, no doubt, was simply *comme il faut*. It is doubtful he would have been quite so forward on his own initiative: it had been Klaus who'd suggested, as he'd gone off with his sister to some Negro dance palace, that he share his evening aperitif with the Leamington's resident waif. Klaus was ever the Leporello. In the once-upon-a-time of München

he would bring home friends from school who'd been invited specially to accommodate what he supposed were his father's tastes.
He (or Erika) would dance with them there in the goodly dining
hall — tangos, polkas, American jazz, like merchants exhibiting
their best wares. How could one not enjoy such a tumble of pup-
pies? Their energy! their wet noses and warm, ingenuous tongues!
their merriment, for what is merrier than drunken children? He
wondered how many Manhattans this one would need before she
was all giggles and sly flirtation.

She approached him, the attendant following with her drink on
his tray of up-to-the-minute American plastic. "Please," he said,
offering his hand limply, as though to be kissed. "Sit here beside
me. We two would seem to have the whole hotel to ourselves. I
am Hermann."

That was, of course, a lie, but it was an official lie, in that he had
been registered at the Leamington as "Hermann Hesse," an irony
he could share with no one but Klaus and Erika. It was quite lost
on their liaison with the FBI, Mr. Steele. As Klaus had jested, in
his ever-more-elegant English, there was no irony in that steel!
Steele seemed never to have read a work of literature in his life, a
proper savage such as he had once supposed (quite unjustly) all
Americans to be.

"Hermann Hesse," he added, not without a twinge at the thought
that with this milkmaid his own name would have produced as little sign of recognition. "But please to call me Hermann."

He took her hand, pressed the limp fingers in a tighter bundle,
and she said, "Chantal."

At first he thought she'd said, "*Enchanté*," and then the drollery
of it dawned: Chantal was her name! She had quite trumped his
ace. Were he to waft her away to Hollywood and put her into the
hands of Fritzl's own press agent, she could not have been more

tellingly repackaged. Just "Chantal," like Ouida or Colette, no last name to suggest the realm of the patriarch.

"Chantal," he repeated. "A charming name. Do, please, have a seat." He gestured for the attendant to place her drink on the low table before them. "And may I ask: what is the book you have been reading with such stern attention?"

"Oh this. It's a bunch of old speeches by that Catholic priest who's on the radio."

Though she spoke dismissively, the book was there on her lap, her index finger marking her place, not easily dismissible. He tipped the book forward so as better to see the cover.

"Oh. Father Coughlin." A shadow seemed to darken the lobby, as though heavy curtains had been drawn. At once he regretted his impulse to become acquainted with an indigene. "Yes, one hears much of him these days."

With a womanly gift for catching the unexpressed emotional weight of a moment, she sensed his disapproval and said, "It really isn't my sort of thing at all. Someone I know wanted me to read it. But I can't really get into it. Myself, I'd rather read a story. If I read anything at all."

"Really? I'm just the same."

Was it just his professional vanity that prompted him to believe that she was not simply sidestepping an unwelcome political argument? There must be, even here so far the Fatherland, milkmaids with a partiality for the *Führer*. He would put it to the test: "And what story have you read lately that you could recommend?"

"Oh gee, that's a hard one." She crimped her brow so that one could almost hear the gears engage. "There's one I kind of liked, but the writer is…controversial. Are you Catholic?"

He shook his head.

"The reason I ask is I know a priest who disapproves of the writer.

Have you ever heard of John Steinbeck?"

"Oh yes."

"Well, there's a book by him, not the long one that just came out, but earlier. *Of Mice and Men*. It's kind of spicy, but that's not why I would recommend it. There's a character in it who reminds me of my brother." She took a quick drink from her Manhattan, as though to erase her last words. "That's not the reason either. It's just a good book. But very sad."

Now might he indeed claim to be *enchanté*. The child was the very princess of all milkmaids, another Zerlina. Here was reason to hope for the coming victory of democracy that was the main tenet of his so-often-unsteady secular faith and the theme of his own perpetual Chautauqua! It was as though one had sat down beside Pocahontas on the shores of the wild Rappahannock and heard her expound, in her own native tongue, the essence of Kant's critique of reason. To sleep with her would be to make love to the entire continent. The Wedding of Europe and America! Oh, how well Klaus knew him! What a little Mephistofeles he was! His Muse who had been so weary, who had almost died in her traces during the long Sisyphean labor of *Lotte*, would live again. She was beside him now, sucking voluptuously on the whiskey-drenched cherry from her drink, and *he* was beside himself! For he could feel his Joseph stir again within his breast, where for so long he'd been buried and despaired of. Joseph, who had been cast into the pit by his own brothers! Joseph, a slave in Egypt, a prisoner in Pharaoh's dungeon! He would live! He would rule in Egypt! And all through this charming Chantal, this Indian maiden, this little movie star, this American sweetie-pie!

Yes! he would have her or his name was not Thomas Mann.

Chapter Four

ONE THING we gods have in common with novelists is *not* pre-destining power. Despite what the sterner determinists have suggested we gods don't command that kind of Svengali-like control over mankind.[8] Indeed, many of them — gods *and* novelists — tend to be boastful about the autonomy of the characters they've created, who possess free will like latter-day Adam and Eves and develop "lives of their own."

On the other hand, we gods, like many novelists, are omniscient. We can see in the dark, as it were, and hear words that modest maidens dast not speak aloud. No bedchamber is secure from our candid camera; no era too remote, no scruple too delicate, no battle too bloody but we are there to shine our light on it, to prod, sniff, and document the whole thing. We — gods *and* novelists — are bloodhounds and tattletales, and the rest of you mere mortals can do nothing but sit there and listen to what we have to say or else simply to bite your lips and turn away.

Which is why, though I surely love my sainted mother, dead now these many years, and would have wanted in an ordinary filial

---

8 And No! Ms. Copyeditor, you may not amend that to "humankind" or "people" or some other gender-neutral substitute. You've meddled too much with my prose already. Stet mankind or get yourself another job! God has spoken.

way to respect her privacy, I must, in my capacity as a god *and* a novelist, share these glimpses of a past she must have supposed was entirely erased from human memory. What do *you* remember, Reader, from the spring of 1939? Can you, like me and the eponymous narrator of *Tristram Shandy*, report on the circumstances of your own conception?[9] You can't, but a god, this god, has seen everything and forgets nothing. Total recall is not always a blessing (just read Proust, if you can), but it's a theological fact of my life.

Doubters have a certain advantage in this respect. They can take Missouri's motto as their own and demand proof of what deities and their spokesmen assert. My namesake Thomas did, and Jesus let him stick his finger in the hole in his side that the lance had made (the same lance that makes a miraculous appearance at the end of Wagner's *Parsifal*). Of course we only have the Scripture's word for that *coup de théâtre*, and the point of our being told about Thomas's doubt is to praise believers for an unquestioning credulity.

Every child must reenact that same crisis of faith at this time of year, and one of the bittersweet delights of parenthood is first inculcating a belief in Santa Claus and inciting a child's innocent avarice for presents, then (before Santa goes bankrupt) unmasking and declaring, "Hey there, little buddy, *I* am Santa." (In much the same way, if you care to think about it, that in this Holy Writ I've revealed myself to be God.) At once as at the *dénouement* of a good mystery, everything is explained, how it is that Santa, up there at the North Pole, knew if you were asleep or awake, naughty or nice; how the cookies got eaten, how he knew just what you wanted — even the footprints by the fireplace (supposing your

---

9 It's annoying to be asked a string of unanswerable questions, but I have my scriptural precedent in all the questions — taunts, really — that Jehovah put to Job.

parents were so well off they had a fireplace).

This little ritual of disenchantment is the paradigm for all religious beliefs — at least among those who worship Mammon and believe that religious conviction is the domain of children (Santa's faithful) and old women, simpletons, and other Jesus freaks. Real men (for instance, Al Pacino, in *The Godfather*) don't believe in God, though they must say they do by way of being respectable. They will, on being confronted with this fact about themselves, protest with more or less vigor. Some will even kill you for such disrespect if they have the opportunity, and can cite apposite passages in the Koran or the Bible as to why your murder is an obligation laid on them by their god.[10]

It is in his Santa Claus aspect that God can be most dangerous, for it is then he is in most danger himself of being revealed as a sham, a kind of hand puppet deployed by his acolytes to tithe, bully, and otherwise flim-flam the weak, the acquiescent, and the faithful. Depending on the ferocity of his priesthood, a god's punishment for heresy or apostasy can be pretty horrific. The Holy Inquisition burned unbelievers at the stake for the blasphemous suggestion that it is the motion of the Earth and not the sun that makes the latter seem to rise in the sky (God's particular demesne) every morning. To this day die-hard fundamentalists in the Bible Belt would serve up the same punishment to biology teachers who so much as mention Charles Darwin and want to make abortion a capital crime, all the while maintaining that it was not their will but God's being done.

In Barryville, our other home, we get the Middletown *Times-*

---

10 The novelist in me can't resist sharing an idea I just had for a story: a pair of four-year-olds who make extortionate demands on Old Nick; then, having provoked their dad to expose himself as the true Santa, decide to poison the glass of milk left out for Santa. The story ends as visions of sugarplums dance in their heads.

Herald Record every day. Not only does it offer news of local crimes and traffic fatalities, but its letter column offers unwitting insights into the minds of local citizens, a large fraction of whom have an inside line on what God wants done in all departments of human behavior. As you might expect, God is against abortion and deplores homosexuality. With regard to the capital punishment and the war in Iraq he seems to incline both ways, depending on who is passing along his wisdom. But whatever position God is advancing, his manner is always recognizably peremptory. He seems unaware that another view than his own might be expressed. The letters written to convey his demands are brief and innocent of any rhetorical strategy but the traditional parental argument, "Because I said so!"

I fear I may be rather like that myself. It seems an unavoidable occupational hazard when one is God. In some respects, I *am* an easy-going divinity. For instance, I don't have any dietary requirements to pass along. Indeed, I might be better off myself if I did. I have tried to cut down on the carbs, and since I learned I was diabetic, I've reduced my sugar intake drastically, but I let my believers have all the leeway they like, calorie-wise. Gather ye rosebuds, it's okay with me.

As to books and movies, it's *chacun à son goût* with this god. My own taste has gotten pickier as I've got older, but yours will too in all likelihood. "While ye may" doesn't necessarily presume death as its limit, in terms of gathering rosebuds. But if you actually enjoy rap music or J. R. R. Tolkien, enjoy!

As for the serious stuff, the things that God's henchmen writing in to the *Times-Herald Record* get most steamed up about, hey, if it's legal this god says "Let your conscience be your guide." (And if it's not, at least be careful.)

But don't think, because like Santa and Silenus I have my merry side, that I am an entirely permissive god and, as Cole Porter has it, anything goes. Not at all.

Let me offer just one commandment as a for-instance: Thou shalt not fight wars. You might say that's not original with me. Moses already included the even terser "Thou shalt not kill" in the tablets of the law that he brought down from Sinai. But the same god who handed those tablets to Moses had him exterminate entire tribes that were sitting on real estate that he wanted for his Chosen People (or so they claimed), and the Middle East has been one bloodbath after another ever since. And it wasn't just in ancient Israel that God allowed exceptions to "Thou shalt not kill." The exceptions have been the rule.

That won't be the case in the covenant I'm drawing up with the human race. When I say "No more war," that's just what I mean, and if someone on the other side of the river ignores my divine law and sends his or her armies *across* the river, my commandment stands. Even to defend your homeland, sanctified by the blood of your forebears, war is not allowed.

"But," you may say, "that's tantamount to suicide!" A good point. It may well be the case that the example of your unresisting and principled pacifism will not be a deterrent to a ruthless and unprincipled enemy who wants to burn your barns and enslave your offspring (if they're that lucky), and destroy your temples. It makes no difference, that's what God demands of you, and you must admit that it's one-up on just turning the other cheek.

Gods do ask a lot. Abraham was told to kill his son, and Jephtha ditto with his daughter. Noah had to go to the expense of that enormous ark, not to mention making a fool of himself before all the neighbors. Pentheus was ripped to shreds by his own deranged mother for not getting drunk on the occasion of Bacchus's annual bacchanal. The list goes on, and the moral of every story is that

God is right and you are wrong.

I find that moral so personally gratifying that, although I hadn't been intending to, I'll end the chapter now.

Think about it. Get the tattoo.

Chapter Five

GODS OF ANY REAL STATURE have a double or even triple nature. Janus had two faces; Jesus (like me) was both man and god, plus he was one of a trinity of gods. All the Greek gods wore disguises from time to time, but a few doubled as major forces of nature. In some ways Apollo was the sun and his sister the moon. Vishnu was the same as the creator Brahma who was the same as Shiva the Destroyer. Even demons have *döppelgangers:* werewolves and body-snatching aliens pass themselves off as just plain folk, and the Evil Queen can curdle at will into the Wicked Witch, a transformation that I found utterly confounding when I first witnessed it with my Aunt Aurelia in the Nokomis Theater on Lake Street in 1944. Perhaps I intuited that the dichotomy of haughty queen/cackling hag was a prefiguration of my own divided self, the Good Tom/Bad Tom of the new age then just getting under way.

The two sides of my divinity are actually not as simple as Good vs. Bad. Dark vs. Light comes closer the mark, and readers of my poetry will already have caught an echo of that in the title of my 1991 collection, *Dark Verses and Light.*[11] In hindsight any number of the poems in that collection can be understood as Holy Writ *avant la lettre,* so to speak. I open the book at random and discover

---

11 *Dark Verses and Light* by Tom Disch (Johns Hopkins, 1991).

these words ascribed to the character of Gladys, in my Masque, "The Eightfold Way," which explicates the mysteries of particle physics:

> *I have this image of myself on a golden throne*
> *Surrounded by a multitude of worshippers,*
> *But whether they're worshipping me or I'm only*
> *A sort of high priestess I can't be sure.*
> *It's not even clear that I'm a woman, I might be a man.*

Sometimes the revelations that the text imparts transcend the realms of particle physics (or extend that realm to the divine), as when Gladys, speaking to Vaslav Nijinsky, speculates:

> *Then there must be another level of being,*
> *Larger than planets or smaller than molecules,*
> *Where the soul may go, as to a dressing room,*
> *To change the clothing of its flesh. Ballet*
> *Is not, not, not about our physicality.*
> *Ballet is love!*

There follows a long duet modeled after the *Liebestod* in *Tristan und Isolde* that shimmers with the most profound intimations of sacred wisdom, which it would be immodest of me to commend at any greater length.

Let me, rather, return to the theme I was pursuing earlier, my double nature. Not so much its human/divine divide but the dichotomy between light and dark. What better time than Yuletide, when the solstice has whittled away our afternoons and night begins at four P.M., to think about the true meaning of Winter?

Not just the threat it poses to all warm-blooded creatures, nor the dreariness of landscapes denuded of their greenery, but its chill, glistening beauty as well. Winter in its Christmas-card aspect, with treetops and rooftops covered with snow and everything simplified to a lesson in geometry by way of reminding us that God is first and foremost a mathematician, then a nuclear physicist, and only at many removes of causation an infant in a manger warmed by the breath of barnyard animals and comforted by the caroling of angels. Then come the wise men with their presents, and then, centuries later, Santa Claus with *his* presents, and finally, the Homer of the American Christmas, Clement Moore, whose poem "A Visit from St. Nicholas," appeared in the Troy, New York *Sentinel* of December 23, 1823.

A still unpublished collection of my poems, *The Moon on the Crest of the New-Fallen Snow*, takes its title from Moore's poem, or I should say "adapts" its title, for Moore actually wrote "The moon on the breast of the new fallen snow,/Gave the lustre of mid-day to objects below." If I'd been his editor at the *Sentinel* I would also have deleted that comma after "snow" and amended "the lustre" to "a lustre." I have always loved that particular couplet, along with another a few lines later, "As dry leaves before the wild hurricane fly,/When they meet with an obstacle, mount to the sky..."[12] Before I wrote "The Moon on the Crest of the New-Fallen Snow,"[13] I'd already determined to make it the title poem of my next and possibly last collection. I knew I wanted that book drenched in *Eau de Nightingale*. So without more ado, here is

---

12 The poet was a little careless here as well, for shouldn't there be a "that" after "dry leaves"? That's how I memorized it, and how it appears in the 1905 anthology, *Heart Throbs* (Grosset & Dunlap).

13 Written on January 27, 1994, and first published in *Paris Review* #135, Summer 1995.

The Moon on the Crest of the New-Fallen Snow

These are those same trees you saw six months ago.
I've drawn them in a way that will explain
Not only their nature, but the nature of snow,
And my own — removed, yet not unaware. Pain

Has its place — and pity, too — but it is not here.
Here all is calm and cold and luminous.
The snow has smoothed over the tracks of the deer.
The moon — I am the moon — would rather be oblivious

Of what lives, since the moon itself is not alive.
It enjoys superior — some might say supernal —
Pleasures. It is confident it can survive
The loss of leaves, of love, of life. Eternal

As the miracle it mirrors, the moon
Transcends, and maps, all circumstances.
It is at midnight as it is at noon.
It sits alone and smiles, as the snow dances.

Let me point out for those unaccustomed to close reading that the "I" of line two is the moon himself, as we learn a few lines later, and so he can be understood to have "drawn" the trees by casting their shadows on the snow. As to my claiming not to be alive, that is one of the prerogatives of poetic license, as much as my claiming to be the moon. In saying "I am the moon," I am making the moon my hand puppet, in much the way I've suggested that people telling stories about the gods make them their hand puppets. The difference, I suppose, is that while poets are concerned to evoke a sense of beauty, evangelists are out to elicit reverence and to command obedience.

When I wrote that poem I was not yet entirely aware of my own divinity, though clearly I had inklings. Indeed, I think it likely I didn't want to *know* that I was God (other than metaphorically), not if I was going to be a god as chilly and impersonal as all that. My inclination in sunnier moments is to come across in a more Falstaffian vein, like jolly old St. Nick himself. As John Donne[14] has written: "By much laughing thou mayst know there is a fool, not that the laughers are fools, but that among them there is some fool at whom wise men laugh"; which moved Erasmus to put this as his first Argument in the mouth of his *Folly*, "that *she made Beholders laugh*; for fools are the most laughed at, and laugh the least themselves of any."

Well, even gods don't get to pick the kind of god they're going to be, any more than poets can choose their muses. Those are for Fate to determine, stern Fate whom even gods obey, and Fate decreed that I should not be very popular in high school. That led me to shed my share of tears, but I grew reconciled to the self I'd been allotted. I may not be the life of the party, no Dionysus, but as an alternative role-model Apollo is surely not to be sneezed at. Of course, I'm not exactly another Apollo either, not in the Best Dressed or Mr. Universe sense, but the kind of lustre I do cast at my best is like the moon's in Moore's poem, a lustre of midday — even though in fact it's actually night. Gods thrive on paradoxes like that.

By the way, I should point out before we leave Yuletide behind us (already, as I write, we are only hours shy of New Year's Eve!) that Clement Moore was not the true author of "A Visit from

---

14 *Paradoxes* x, "That a Wise Man is Known by Much Laughing" by John Donne.

St. Nicholas." The true author was Major Henry Livingston, Jr; Moore, a much inferior poet, took credit for the poem after it first appeared anonymously in 1823. It was only ascribed to Moore in 1836, when Livingston was already dead. Moore acquiesced in the expropriation,[15] and thereby entered literary history and the Library of America.

But enough of midnight's uncanny beauty. As I said at the very beginning of my creation: Let there be light! I might add, in Milton's immortal words, "Come thou goddess fair and free,/ In heav'n yclept Euphrosyne." Would you believe that as a junior at Central High School in St. Paul, I memorized both "L'Allegro" and "Il Penseroso" in their entirety — and did so almost involuntarily. Its couplets just glued themselves to my memory like those strips of cellophane tape that grab hold of anything that gets too near. These days I couldn't accomplish such a feat to save my soul. When I tried to memorize Robert Frost's "Provide! Provide!" two years ago, so that I might reel it off on the right occasion, it would not stick.

I mention this not to reveal that God has feet of clay but as prelude to yet another piece of bragging — that another poet has memorized the ballade with which I'd like to close this chapter, and has recited it on numerous occasions along with poems of his own. That personage is none other than the Chairman of the National Endowment for the Arts, Dana Gioia! How's that for a feather in my cap? I haven't actually been present for one of Dana's recitations. Indeed, I haven't seen him since he assumed his chairmanship, just as he's not seen me since I revealed my mission here on Earth, but I like to think that his recitations of the poem represent a tacit acknowledgement of its message.

---

15 The crime is investigated in detail in *Author Unknown: On the Trail of Anonymous* by Don Foster (Henry Holt, 2000), and Moore's claims are not left a leg to stand on.

"Ballade of the New God" represents my first public proclamation of my divinity, and as such it is a poem of universal significance. What more can I say? — except

Ballade of the New God

I have decided I'm divine.
Caligula and Nero knew
A godliness akin to mine,
But they are strictly hitherto.
They're dead, and what can dead gods do?
I'm here and now. I'm dynamite.
I'd worship me if I were you.
A new religion starts tonight!

No booze, no pot, no sex, no swine:
I have decreed them all taboo.
My words will be your only wine,
The thought of me your honeydew.
All other thoughts you will eschew.
You'll call yourself a Thomasite
And hymn my praise with loud yahoo.
A new religion starts tonight.

But (you might think) that's asinine!
I'm just as much a god as you.
You may have built yourself a shrine,
But I won't bend my knee. Who
Asked you to be my god? I do
Who am, as god, divinely right.
Now you must join my retinue:

A new religion starts tonight.

All that I have said is true.
I'm god and you're my acolyte.
Surrender's bliss: I envy you.
A new religion starts tonight.

Chapter Six

AS I'VE ALREADY NOTED EARLIER, gods are great ones for masquerading. The Holy Ghost descends as a dove; Zeus on a similar mission visited the lovely Io in the form of a cloud. (Correggio gave a scrumptious account of that close encounter.) Even when they're not trying to conceal their divine identities, gods like fancy clothes, if we're to trust the paintings they appear in. I am no different.

My favorite form of fancy dress has always been western wear. At the age of twelve I used to clip out the ads for Levi's jeans from *Life* and use them for my own devotional purposes. I got a really snazzy cowboy shirt when I was fourteen, pink and black with fringe and pearl snaps (Whoopee!), though I never dared wear it to school. As for boots and rodeo-sized belt buckles and wide-brimmed Stetsons, those glories had to wait until I had escaped the Twin Cities for New York City, where the deer and the antelope play and one seldom hears a discouraging word. (Discouraging words were rife in Minnesota.)

I never got to meet any real cowboys until just after age eighteen when I was locked up in an army brig with a guy my own age who was really good looking, played chess at my own earnest, mediocre level, and confided in me how he intended to murder his father the minute he got discharged from the army. I don't remember the guy's name, but I was in thrall to such Dostoyevskian pizzazz. I didn't feel an equal reverence for the Mormans (Mormons) who were my neighbors in Amecameca six years later, but the hunkier one of them competed in rodeos and had the scars to prove it. There was no doubt who was the alpha male in that patio.

I'm sure I'm not alone in my conviction that if Jesus had put off his incarnation for two thousand years or so (as I have), he would have delivered homilies about the Good Cowboy rather than the Good Shepherd, and our calendar art would be radically sexier. Stories about lost sheep can as easily concern themselves with cattle. I've worked with cattle myself, though I rode a tractor rather than a horse and spent more time baling hay than dealing directly with the cows and heifers. Still, it was hands-on experience and should count for something in terms of rooting my worship in the American Experience and the Myth of the West.

As much as I admire western wear I don't think I will make it a required component of my worship, like yarmulkes or burqas. Sideburns, chaps, and six shooters will be optional. The reason I bring them up at all is that they are *emblems* of a side of the American way of faith that is very much to the point of the worship I hope to inspire myself, and there is no better way to unfold the deeper meaning those emblems embody than to include the following parable[16] from two decades ago in the body of my Holy Writ.

---

16 "The New Me" first appeared in *Changes*, edited by Michael Bishop and Ian Watson (Ace, 1983).

The New Me

"Close your eyes now," said Dr. Schencker. "It's night, you're tired, and we're not here to discuss reality. Reality's boring and much too painful. We're concerned with your *needs*. Now ever so slowly you're drifting away, you're out of control, you're out of control, you're a zombie. How do you feel?"

"Wide awake, I'm afraid," I replied.

"You *think* you're wide awake," he said, somewhat testily. "In fact, you're in deep hypnotic trance. Repeat that."

"In fact I'm in a deep hypnotic trance. But it doesn't feel like it. There was never even a spell when I was drowsy."

"Mr. Gulbradsen, you must be more cooperative. It's *your* job that's at stake. If you don't make the effort that's required, you'll be out on the street: the Director of Personnel left no doubt of that. Now — do you want a new personality or don't you?"

"It's not a question of what *I* want, really. It's my students. They don't like me and as a result, it seems, they're unwilling to learn anything from me. Actually, I doubt if my personality has much to do with it one way or the other. They've told themselves in advance they can't understand math, so they don't try. None of them want to be structural-steel draughtsmen, for which I can't blame them, since there aren't any jobs for them once they're out of the training program. If there *were*, believe me, I wouldn't be tutoring terminally unemployable dropouts in trigonometry. I'd take the job myself. That's *my* assessment of the situation."

"Yet the classes of other teachers consistently score better than yours. How do you account for that?"

"Cynicism on the part of the other teachers. They're not teaching math, just a procedure for thumbing through *Smoley's New Combined Tables*. A pigeon could do that, with practice."

"Then show your students as much consideration as you would a pigeon and teach them that procedure. But first, of course, you must make them listen to you, and I gather there has been some resistance on their part to doing so. Little wonder, I should say. You fairly radiate defeat, Mr. Gulbradsen. Your suit is the contemporary equivalent of sackcloth and ashes. You walk like a pallbearer. Your smile is eighty percent sneer. Where is the joy of life? Where is the appetite, aggression, energy?"

"Yes. Well. I thought you said we wouldn't discuss reality."

"I'd like to make a strong post-hypnotic suggestion, Mr. Gulbradsen. The company offers an Assertiveness Training group every Thursday at 6:30 in 'D' Conference Room. Be there. And Sensitivity is on Friday — you might as well go to that too."

What could I do? I didn't want to be fired. I went. I learned the recommended techniques for assertiveness and sensitivity, and I followed all of Dr. Schencker's post-hypnotic suggestions. I changed my name, my clothes, my habits, my opinions. I developed a more sincere smile and a stronger handshake. One Friday night I went on a marathon crying jag, following which I had a short but intense affair with one of the secretaries I'd impressed by my openness and vulnerability. I taught myself to drawl in basic Miss-to-Mex style, like NBC's Marshall Jack. On weekends I attended rodeos, square dances, and barbecues.

As a result of my new behavior patterns my life changed much along the lines the doctor had predicated. My students paid closer attention (if only, I supposed, for my oddity) and got better exam scores. I formed a new circle of friends, chiefly among other men who dressed in western apparel. Professionally they were a varied lot: two accountants, a dentist, a labor racketeer, and an advertising copywriter. They were also, like me, on the heavy side.

Everything seemed to be functioning smoothly, and then I made the mistake of telling Dr. Schencker about my doubts as to the authenticity of this way of life. I suspected that all my new acquaintances were acting as they did because they were in Assertiveness Training too. He assured me that what I needed was a lesson in Basic Trust and Self-Confidence, and gave me a card that for a ten percent discount at a skydiving school that would teach me these lessons. As an inducement he promised me that after my first jump I wouldn't have to take any more therapy. I'd be considered a completed job.

Three weeks later I was back on his couch, in complete abjection, a dropout from my jump school. "Close your eyes now," the doctor told me. "We're going deep, deep into your psychic sub-basement, right to the bottom where your parents' bones are buried. I'll count to three, and then you'll tell me exactly why you chickened out at the moment of truth. All right one, two, three."

"Ah did not chicken out," I repeated. "Ah told yahl what happened. Ah went up in the plane. Ah was standing in line with mah parachute, and then the man raht in front of me jumps out with a big 'Yahoo!' just lahk they taught us — and jumped raht out of his parachute too."

"That is unfortunate, surely, but it wasn't likely to happen to you."

"Ah was not about to take the chance. The people who run that operation were criminally negligent. Do I have to commit suicide in order to show my Basic Trust to a bunch of murderers?"

"Accent, accent," Dr. Schencker reminded me.

"Mah Basic cotton-pickin' Trust — how's that?"

"No need to be sarcastic. The fact remains, Tex, you haven't solved your problem. While the people who did make that jump have achieved some real personal growth."

"Ah wonder sometimes, Doc, whether mah problem is not having Basic Trust in other people. Ah mean, maybe a person *should* be alienated some of the time, maybe some people don't *deserve* our trust."

"You're resisting again," said the doctor, and reached under his desk to press a button that broadcast a mild electric shock to my pleasure center. I flinched. "Though possibly skydiving is not the right approach in your case. Maybe the right angle for you would be Faith. Your Minnesota Multiphasic would suggest that you have intensely religious personality structure."

"Ah doubt that somehow, Doc. Ah mean, for one thing Ah'm an atheist, like my pappy before me and his pappy before him."

"Then you've been stifling your natural disposition. I suggest, Tex, that you accept Christ as your personal savior and get born again." He snapped his fingers in my face. "All right — wake up!"

I blinked my eyes. "Are we through?" He liked me to pretend that I couldn't remember anything that went on in our sessions.

The next Sunday I drove down Route 17, checking out the prices of the various religious chapels and tabernacles that specialized in the process of rebirth. Lacking established preferences, I finally settled on Noah's Ark Pentecostal Mission and Children's Zoo, whose gigantic billboard — an elephant holding up a placard saying SAVE AND BE SAVED — offered the lowest rates in the city for baptism by total immersion. Despite this there were only three other cars in the mission's parking lot, one of which seemed to have been abandoned rather than parked. Its front tires were flat, its windshield speckled with bird droppings, and graffiti was scrawled in the dust that coated it — DARN, GOSH, HECK.

Inside the mission an elderly usher showed me into a kind of locker room and told me to prepare for baptism. I changed into swim trunks and waited. The sound system wheezed jungle noises — cockatoos, monkeys, the howls and roars of far-off predators — for the benefit, presumably, of visitors to the zoo.

Then the jungle vanished and the loudspeaker crackled into speech. "Mr. Gilbertson?"

"Just call me Tex," I said from habit.

"Welcome to the Noah's Ark Mission, Tex. We are sorry for this momentary inconvenience. Reverend Billy will be along soon. In the meantime, perhaps you'd like to go through the red door — do you see it — and step into the jacuzzi. Thank you for your cooperation and God bless you." The voice ended with a click and the jungle tape was resumed.

The room behind the red door was not much larger than a closet and smelled strongly of disinfectant. Contact paper in a pattern of pink enamel tiles clung to and warped away from the crumbly plastic walls. The narrow space was lighted by a 15-watt amber bulb.

The sound system repeated, verbatim, its invitation to enter the jacuzzi, but I still hesitated. The two scant inches of water, rimed with meringue-like scuzz, were a powerful dissuasion.

A short, stocky woman in a two-piece swimsuit and a Dolly Parton wig entered the baptism cubicle. "Howdy," she twanged in a friendly way. "I'm Reverend Billy, and I understand you've found Jesus and you want your sins to be washed away. Hallelujah. Is that right, Tex?"

"Um, basically, yes."

"Let me ask you one question, Tex, and then we'll — Oh, drat! Grandpa hasn't filled the tub. This is going to take a little longer than I thought. We can't achieve total immersion in that bitty puddle, can we?"

She turned on the tap and water swirled into the tub, making spiral patterns of the meringue. Reverend Billy led me back into the locker room, where she plopped down on a bench beside her discarded clothes. "Cigarette?" she asked, removing a pack from the pocket of her pants suit. Too late I realized I had accepted a menthol cigarette. I hate the taste of menthol.

"Well, Tex—" Reverend Billy released a contented puff of smoke. "— let me tell you something about our faith here at the Mission. Like all good Christian people we believe in Jesus Christ and a Day of Judgment when the dead will rise up and all such as that. I gather we're agreed on that."

I nodded.

"But we've got another, extra belief that sort of sets us apart and makes us a little special. We believe every word of Chapters 7 and 8 in Genesis, how the waters of the flood prevailed upon the Earth a hundred and fifty days, and how all the other living creatures drowned excepting only the animals Noah had saved. And we believe that all animals in the world today — from the bittiest mouse to big old elephants — are descended from the animals on Noah's Ark. Now can you believe that, Tex — sincerely and literally and without fibbing?"

"Well, Reverend Billy, Ah'll have to give that some thought."

While I thought, the animals in the jungle hooted and screeched.

"I suppose," Reverend Billy said, "that you've been brainwashed at one of these modern schools that teach about Darwin and that evolution stuff."

"Ah have read Darwin, yes, ma'am."

"Well, you can forget about Darwin, Tex. The way it happened is the way it says right there in the Holy Bible. I want you to believe that. Do you?"

"Um…sure."

"Sounds like you're just *saying* that, Tex. Sounds like deep down inside you don't really believe it at all."

"You're certainly not helping me very much, Reverend. Ah *said* Ah believed."

"You got to add 'Hallelujah!' or something like that. You got to sound like a believer. Now I know you probably don't believe none of that stuff about Noah, spite of anything you say. Not many people can swallow that one anymore. That's why we settled on Noah's Ark as a special test, plus the fact that Grandpa's got a magic touch with the animals."

"But…um…Ah find that a mite confusing."

"Oh, it's simple enough. If you can look someone right in the eye and say 'Damn straight, I believe in Noah's Ark!' then there's not going to be many other cowpokes around who'll want to mess with *you*. Nosiree. They'll be thinking, '*Keerist*, this *hombre* is *dangerous*.' Faith can be a powerful weapon, Tex. Like Jesus says, 'I came not to send peace, but a sword.'"

"Ah think Ah'm beginning to get the drift. In many ways you learn the same lesson in ordinary Assertiveness Training."

"So I've been told. But this is Religion, Tex, and it requires a bigger personal commitment. You got to come in once a week, if you want to *stay* born-again, and help us parading the animals around the tabernacle. If you got kids, bring 'em — they all love to ride. Then you got to pledge ten percent of your income, but if you fiddle your taxes right it's nearly an equal trade-off. Finally it would be nice if you could learn to yodel. For some reason I never understood this has always been a big congregation for yodeling. Now let's see if that tub is full yet."

She went into the cubicle and turned off the water, dropping ashes from her cigarette into the tub as she did so. She slapped my rump affably. "Climb in! And while I'm baptizing you, I want you to be thinking about the Almighty and this beautiful world He's made for us to have dominion over."

I squatted down, legs bent double, into the lukewarm water and took a deep breath. Reverend Billy placed her hands squarely on my shoulders and said, "Close your eyes now," and pushed me down till the water was over my head. She'd pushed too soon and I'd got water up my nose. Spluttering, I signaled her to release me but her grip was strong and steady. My legs had slipped up out of the water and flailed helplessly in the air. In alarm I opened my eyes and goggled, through the lens of agitated water, at Reverend Billy's resolute face as she went on baptizing me with judicially deliberate speed. Just as, in my panic, I'd come to believe she intended to drown me, Reverend Billy released her grip and I pulled myself up, choking, out of the water.

"You've been saved," she announced matter-of-factly.

"Hallelujah," I answered. "Bless the Lord."

Since that time I have never been troubled by doubts or mental reservations. I know that Jesus loves me, I believe in Noah's Ark, and I have complete confidence in my own future success. This faith has been borne out by significant pay-boosts and the promise of a big promotion just around the corner. I'm a completely different person from the person I used to be, and very dangerous.

I don't mean to suggest [speaking as the god Tom Disch again, and not as Tex] that I shall require a belief in Noah's Ark as a test of orthodox belief. I think we can agree that proponents of creationist "science" are *infra dig*, intellectually speaking. As well ask people nowadays to believe in a Ptolemaic universe. What I do admire in the born-again Tex, and in cowboys generally, is that they are tough motherfuckers whom other people do not want to mess with. Whether they appear at PTA meetings to denounce satanic science textbooks,[17] or aim their bazookas at abortion clinics, they are scary, and don't we all want to make our enemies afraid of us?

Strange clothes will do that (and not just cowboy clothes, but simple headscarves if you are a French schoolgirl, or turbans and weird beards if you're a Sikh), and so will odd alphabets and dead languages. I knew two heroin addicts, back in the sixties, who made lavish use of hieroglyphics by way of giving their addiction an aura of arcane spirituality. But a bonkers, off-the-wall, in-your-face affirmation of some really dumb idea works better than anything else. Some gurus feel the need to invent their own lunatic ideas (Mormons and Scientologists have some lulus and they'll sue the shit out of anyone who so much as smiles in their direction), but the most convenient and popular form of divine madness is still that old time religion.

How shall those who have placed their faith in me achieve similar notoriety and have the same kind of mischievous fun as our fundamentalist fellow citizens? One simple tactic would be to insist that this book be ordered by your local library, or, better yet, your local *school* library. When the librarian declines your request, make a stink. Take your cue from the creationists and invoke the First Amendment.

But stop short of creating so large a nuisance that you could get arrested. No religion is worth that kind of trouble.

---

17 "Satan himself is the originator of the concept of evolution," wrote Henry M. Morris, the editor of *Scientific Creationism* (public school edition, Creation-Life Publishers, 1974).

Chapter Seven

HEAVEN.

In a perfect world, or if I were a smart-ass like Laurence Sterne, I might just leave it at that and let my readers infer, after a moment's puzzlement, that not another word were needed. But that's not the way Holy Writs get written.

Heaven is an article of faith in most of my competitors' religions, because faith is a function of desire, and everyone wants to go to heaven, the way all kids want to go to Disneyland. It's not just the advertising — not in Heaven's case, at least — it's the way we're all hardwired to our pleasure centers and can't get enough of a good thing. Rats will starve to death rather than waste their time eating, if their choice is between food and a zap of pure ding-a-ling pleasure. Ditto crack heads. Religions, of course, usually find a politer way to portray and promote our last reward. Sister Fidelis, back in Fairmont, Minnesota, explained that heaven's greatest pleasure was just sitting there in God's presence and contemplating His majesty. She made it sound like Friday night novenas when Father Lane held up the monstrance with the Holy Eucharist in it, but on an astronomical scale. Put that way, heaven didn't seem a compelling reason to exert oneself in other than painless pro forma ways like brushing one's teeth and wearing clean underwear.

Muslims look forward to a heaven whose delights are much more alluring. They are promised an afterlife of pure ice cream by their imams, especially if they've proven themselves to be martyrs for their faith. In that case, once they've slain their quota of infidels, each martyr is guaranteed seventy virgins for an eternity of orgasmic pleasure. How those virgins may conduct themselves, what they will wear, how they will spell each other at their task of endless, insatiable pleasure-giving has not been widely discussed in the literature I've read. Perhaps each Muslim martyr decides those things for himself, or perhaps the protocols of the heavenly orgy are imparted in special X-rated prayer meetings at the mosque.[18] In any case, it's been a very successful system of incentives. Perhaps the martyrs of 9/11 might have leveled the World Trade Center without the enticement of the seventy virgins — just from a sense for sheer envy, resentment, and spite. Perhaps their operative motive was piety. We can only guess.

I don't want to give the impression that I'm a member of the Anti-Sex League or that my own orgasms have been of such poor quality that I undervalue the pleasure principle. There's nothing like a good fuck, unless it's another good fuck. But can anyone sustain their wild ecstasies through eternity? That's the question theologians must ask themselves. There comes a point, orgasmically speaking, when we all poop out and want no more than a cigarette and then to watch the smoke wreathing up into the light. Such a mood of sated contemplative peace offers an alternative scale-model of the divine bliss we may enjoy hereafter.

That is to say, Art.

---

18 Perhaps it is no coincidence that the staff of most heterosexually-oriented video porn shops are young Arab-speaking men. Their work in the American porn industry may be understood as a kind of missionary effort akin to the work of young Mormons in Mexico and the Irish and Italians all over Africa.

No art in particular, or rather any of them, will serve as a paradigm of a happy afterlife. Even dance, that most carnal of the arts, has its versions of heaven, from all the chorus lines in all the versions of "I'll Build a Stairway to Paradise" to ballet's own Sistine Chapel, the second act of *Giselle*, where the ethereal willies perform their eternal twinkle-toed perambulations, which I've always figured was heaven enow.

However, as a metonym for heaven, dance has the same drawback as orgasm. It's tiring. After the ball one may sing "I could have danced all night" — but all night and then the next day, and the week following, and through all eternity? Not even Julie Andrews could make such a boast. In fact ceaseless dancing is the punishment meted out to the villain in *Giselle*.

So forget Terpsichore. Try architecture, and ecclesiastical architecture in particular. Any church or temple or mosque is a scale model of the heaven in which the faithful hope to assemble in the afterlife. Just look up inside the domes of St. Mark's Basilica in Venice or the Baptistry in Florence, and there, bigger than life, in a heaven of gold tesserae, is God and, on a smaller scale, his angels, very much the way Sister Fidelis had promised, all calm and bright and ready to be adored. The only difficulty from a practical viewpoint is that if those in the nave try to emulate the level, everlasting gaze of the saints and angels on the ceiling they'll get a sore neck. You might try lying down on the floor if the place isn't too crowded and the sacristan takes tips. And (a bigger if) if your own appetite for art history is that voracious. Later churches, especially of the Baroque and Rococo eras, offer trippier heavens of high-resolution illusionism with cloudscapes as billowy as any you will see from the window of a jumbo jet and angels singing *Glory halleluia!* at altitudes and in attitudes no ballerina could rival. No hotel of any age, however gilded, can beat those heavens for sheer deluxe accommodations, and I don't plan any Reformation in that regard. I can promise the worshippers at the Disch Paradiso suites with hot tubs and kitchenettes, with ocean views *and* Alpine vistas from the balcony. You just have to believe in me and wait till you're dead.

Some of the more liberal Protestants these days, and even a few Catholics, claim not to believe in a literal heaven like the Disch Paradiso, with cumulus mattresses and caroling angels. For them heaven is a metaphor for a state of mind outside the ordinary monad by monad flow of daily life, not so much a destination in the Disneyland sense as a state of mind. By the same token Eternity is not just our usual Now with its run indefinitely extended. Eternity collapses all time zones, past, present, and future, into one all-inclusive nanosecond like the Big Bang. Sounds like a lot of malarkey? Yes, but that's the way with all High Art when you peek behind the curtains.

That's probably the chief reason why I am God — and the President of General Motors is not. As Tosca sings, I've lived for art, for all of them, for all my life. I was studying ballet in high school, and the moment I got my diploma I set off with a small troop of intending ballet dancers[19] for the Emerald City of New York. I wasn't intending a career in ballet myself, but I was able to ride on my friends' coattails to jobs as a spear carrier for the Bolshoi (*Spartacus*), the Royal Ballet (*Swan Lake*), and the Metropolitan Opera (*Don Giovanni, Tosca,* etc.). So even if I'd succeeded in my suicide attempt at age eighteen I would not have died in vain.

Instead of persisting in suicide I decided to become an archi-

19 None of them wound up with careers in ballet, but one of them became Robert Joffrey's lover, another (who was straight) teased along Anthony Tudor for two years of chaste snuggling, and a third got to be the leading dancer of a children's dance theater till she got pregnant and left New York in defeat.

tect. I aced the entrance exam for Cooper Union (someone who worked in the office told me I'd got the highest ever score on their entrance test, but maybe that's what she told everyone), then dropped out after a few weeks. My excuse was indigence, but the truth of the matter was that I was never cut out to be an architect. The hammer-and-nails side of the business did not grab me. I had no urge to build houses or even Swiss chalets. My interest was primarily cathedrals, and even at the age of eighteen I sensed that commissions for erecting cathedrals would be hard to come by, especially for a pauper from the provinces. Later, touring Europe, I sated myself on cathedrals, and one of the major pleasures of a stay at the Disch Paradiso is a tour of all the cathedrals ever built, or even well-imagined, in the course of human history, but with special attention to Gothic cathedrals, for in Gothic cathedrals heaven is not illustrated (as on the dome of St. Mark's) but exemplified. I will elaborate on that point when we are all in Amiens together.

Literature was the next fine art on my c.v. I've already pointed out how novelists and gods have similar job descriptions, but I didn't note those ways in which the two jobs are *not* much alike. Writing fiction is a sedentary business. Ballet and building cathedrals require exertions that are physically and spiritually aerobic. You may feel tired when the week's work is over, but you feel god-like, too.

Shakespeare brags that his sonnets will outlast monuments, and Keats credits poetry as a realm of gold, but even Keats, when he's looking for something comparable to heaven doesn't suggest a library. Instead, he poses the question

> *Souls of poets dead and gone,*
> *What Elysium have ye known —*

> *Happy field or mossy cavern*
> *Choicer than the Mermaid Tavern?*

We all want more from heaven than noble thoughts and re-fined sentiments. We want good wine and venison pasties, not to mention (the poet implies) an agreeable female companionship, whether barmaid or mermaid.

Perhaps Elysium and heaven are two different addresses, one earthy, the other otherwise. Joy, in Schiller's ode and Beethoven's symphony, is the daughter of Elysium, and while there is nothing X-rated in those works, they do have a tavernish sort of lilt. In my own poem that took "Elysium" as its title,[20] I describe a des-tined happy tryst in the Elysian meadows of a wino whose tan-gled hair is "the soul's own dirt," and an ancient grande dame who wears "tiara-like, her skull upon her brow." Taverns are, like heav-ens, places where all walks of life converge. The use of alcohol and other recreational drugs has been one of the major bones of con-tention between myself and those gods and prophets who insist on teetotaling. I promise my worshippers a heaven with a selec-tion of good wines by the glass and a juke box with infinite vari-ety.

Which reminds me that I haven't even mentioned music's claims as the art most at home in heaven. Just this past week I've seen on TV the deathless simulacra of Callas and Bartoli, stars of Bollywood and the Grand Ole Opry, the Berlin Philharmonic, and Bob Hoskins, Gemma Craven, and Cheryl Campbell lip-synching their way through *Pennies from Heaven.*

That word again! It seems to infect all references to music like a computer virus, and little wonder, for music, like heaven itself, is

---

20 In *Parnassus*, Vol. xx.

at once immaterial and yummy. Rock walls are leveled and savage beasts are soothed by the sounds of Orpheus's lyre. For all that, I must confess that *this* god remains a mere listener, happy to pay the wages of the angelic choirs (though not always, alas, the price of tickets to the Met) but not myself a participant.

The art in which I have been an enthusiastic amateur, and the one that takes us closest to heaven's door, is painting. I've already spoken of how certain frescos offer gorgeous replicas of heaven, not just the billowing cloudland inhabited by the triple god of Christianity and his wingèd choirs, but such related areas as Olympus, Parnassus, Elysium, and Paradise. But such depictions of the exact spot are far from the only way that painting shares in my original *Fiat Lux!* In her own way Helen Frankenthaler can be every bit as heaven-bent as Tiepolo or other literalist set-designers. Indeed, for those who have a knack for leaping *into* a painting's space as into a swimming pool, Frankenthaler's canvases are the broadest of portals into painterly heaven. The only problem is, one needs a handful of magic seaweed to be able to breathe inside a Frankenthaler.[21]

Whether a painting is abstract or *trompe-l'œil* is irrelevant in terms of its c.i., or Celestial Index. Painters have painted angels who have a c.i. in the low twenties, while others have painted flower pots or fields of wheat whose c.i.s are out of the ballpark. Like the gift of grace in traditional theology you've either got it or you don't. Calvin and other predestinarians extended that cruel logic to the afterlife: you either are admitted into heaven or

---

21 That may need a footnote. In my own manger days there was a Saturday morning radio program, "Land of the Lost," about a fish, Red Lantern, who befriends two children and takes them about his subterranean homeland by giving them each a handful of magic seaweed, which serves them as gills so that like Red Lantern they can breathe under water. I got my magic seaweed when I saw the Helen Frankenthaler retrospective at the Whitney in 1969. Before then her paintings seemed just so much linen soaked in pastel dyes, but with the magic seaweed in my hand, oh my!

you're not. Of course, most Calvinists were of the opinion that they *would* be among the happy few who got past the bouncers at the gate, an assumption that non-Calvinists have been inclined to question. Wars have resulted from that disagreement.

In the interest of avoiding future wars of similar fierceness and duration, I will unfold a mystery. There *is* no heaven — and you can get there by a simple program of diet, exercise, and prayer. But first you must promise *not* to go to war. If you're already in the armed forces that might be an inconvenience, but surely an eternity of endless bliss is worth some small sacrifice. I'm not asking that you give up other gods you may have before you — Jesus, Wotan, Ba'al, whomever — only that you entertain the hypothesis of my divinity as a hypothetical, the way Catholics and even Mormons can practice yoga without being denounced for heresy. Of course, if you're the kind of fundamentalist who gets her dander up over the issue of children trick-or-treating at Halloween, then I don't think I can help you get to heaven. But if you are that sort, you probably haven't got this far in my Holy Writ anyhow. (Your children are another matter; your children are probably ripe for any heresy they can get their hands on. And like Jesus I do suffer little children to come unto me. They need magic seaweed more than anyone.)

As to other gods, and whether they'll be jealous and resent my revelations, I doubt it. All gods these days are aware that most believers hedge their faith with a variety of quibbles and ambivalences. I am always asking friends, and even strangers, whether they believe in a literal afterlife, either a sunny heaven or a fiery hell, and while they can appear miffed at having been put on the spot that way, most allow as how heaven for them is a metaphor. One of the most emphatic such declarations was that of Lois Dodd, a painter whose smallest pochades bespeak a firsthand acquaintance with Paradise.

To say that heaven is a metaphor by no means diminishes its practical potency as a talisman and passkey to secret wisdom. Just ask St. Mary of Egypt in Crespi's wonderful altarpiece. There she is at death's door, in the arms of the angel who will soon bear her away, her lips parted to receive the Eucharist. Do you think she gives a lick about debates over the Transubstantiation? Or Election and Free Will? No, her hunger is not for eternity but for five minutes more, just five minutes more of that angel's arms. That's her heaven and the heaven I can offer all my believers and the heaven I am hasting to myself.

Chapter Eight

GODS HAVE BEEN RATHER GENEROUS in allowing reporters and other interested parties to have a look at hell. They'd be fools not to, for sticks can be more potent motivators than carrots. Greek and Roman poets have left vivid accounts of the torments of Prometheus, of Sisyphus and Tantalus and Ixion, et al., while Dante's *Inferno* is a virtual Rand McNally of the underworld. Milton was somewhat vaguer as to geography and the range of punishments available, but of all literary hells his is surely the most awe-inspiring, to the degree that one might be tempted to go there just to marvel at the sights.

The visual arts, too, have produced some dynamite versions of hell and of the sadistic tricks Satan's minions can get up to. Every medieval cathedral had its doorway with a sculpted version of the Last Judgment, and in the Renaissance the same theme filled ever vaster stretches of frescoed walls until Michelangelo filled the Sistine Chapel with the Last Judgment to end all Last Judgments. To this day hell and damnation are a favorite theme of carnival sideshows all over the world.

Whether the venue is Buchenwald or Abu Ghraib or hell, there is simply no denying the delight we all enjoy in witnessing the whipping, flaying, evisceration, crucifixion, and general ill treatment of our enemies — and our friends and relations, as well. That's why child abuse has been a problem since the days of King Herod, and why child abusers have such a rough time when they're sent to prison. (They won't have such a nice time in hell, either, not if I have anything to say about it.)

Students of Dante like to point out that in his system of poetic justice each sinner's suffering is, in some sense, self-inflicted. It's not just that the punishment fits the crime in Dante's hell; in some higher, allegorical sense it *is* the crime. The adulterous Paolo and Francesca are whirled about in a fiery tornado that is the objective correlative of their guilty love. The great thing about this view of hell's horrors as an allegory is that it lets readers off the hook with regard to their own (possibly sadistic) motives.

I hope my own readers will take the same indulgent view when they read the following account of the sufferings that the science-fiction writer Philip K. Dick has been undergoing in a hell that is in no way *my* creation, but rather the inner truth of his own soul as, inexorably, his sins came home to roost.

A Ranch House on the Styx

Either time itself was a little weird here in the underworld or else *he* was wired or both. He felt as though he'd been dead forever, but if the radio could be trusted this was only the year 2000 and everyone up on Earth was still waiting to learn who'd won the election in Florida and would therefore be the next president, a decision that had been pending since at least Joycelin's last trip to the mall for groceries. Which meant that he'd been dead a little over eighteen years.

Lord knows he looked like he'd been dead that long. Despite Joycelin's best efforts with the scissors and some touching up with Just for Men, his beard and 'stache had gone all scrofulous, and there was some kind of fungoid growth under his right eye as hardy as a dandelion. He would tweezer it out and it would reappear overnight bigger than ever. Did tumors have their own posthumous vitality like hair?

Men! the telepathic radio declared in its most unctuous tone. *Do you worry about progressive hair loss? Does your love life leave something to be desired? Then take a tip from West Anaheim Guns and Ammo: Blow your brains out with a gun from our wide-ranging and up-to-the-minute selection of weapons for those with nothing more to lose! Remember: when alcohol is not enough, West Anaheim has got the stuff! Just take the Kurt Cobain Expressway to Exit 13 and continue to Shadow Valley Mall.* The message was followed by a single gunshot and then the regular programming was resumed.

— Oh yeah! thought Phil, with a reproachful glance at the radio.
— Just try!

He had, many times and many ways. He'd leapt off bridges into the Styx and Acheron; he'd got drunk and gone to sleep in the garage with the Rambler's motor running; he'd taken two brimming tablespoons of roach powder as though it were Metamucil; he'd slit his wrists; and he had followed the ad's advice and gone to Shadow Valley Mall and bought a replica of a huge Civil War handgun and put a bullet through his head. The result, or, rather, results? He'd bobbed up out of the water covered in shit; he'd woken up with a headache; he'd got diarrhea; his wrists itched for weeks; and he'd permanently destroyed his ability to play backgammon — one of the few pleasures left to him in hell — when he could find someone calm enough to play. It just isn't possible to kill yourself once you are dead, and all the ads you heard for bare bodkins or assisted suicide were just so many menu offerings for poor saps like himself. Another Tantalus salivating at the smell of death.

It had been just the same in real life. All his suicide attempts had come to nothing then, as well. The "accident" in '64 when, unable to bear any more of Grania's nagging, he'd flipped the car (he'd been immobilized; she wasn't scratched; the vw was totaled). The games of Russian roulette, both with and without Stelazine. His would-be overdose in '71 when he'd thought the bank had foreclosed. Maybe there'd been others, since he'd come out of more than one gray-out during the bad years with his .22 beside the bed and no memory of how it had got there.

Just thinking about this shit was getting him down, and the view of the Styx at half past six was no help either, with the fumes rolling in over the dead lawns of the development, and nothing in the house to eat but six cans of Alpo. What he needed was something to lift him up out of the pit he was in. If not a crane then some good old-fashioned bennies. The one good thing you could say about hell was that, just as in Orange County, such assistance was always available. If he couldn't blow his brains out with the help of West Anaheim Guns and Ammo, another product could be found to do the job.

Holding on to that purpose, he levered himself up out of his busted La-Z-Boy and crossed the frayed and cat-stained carpet to the phone. But Joycelin was already on the line talking about the election and how the vote had gone in hell and what a shame hell's millions were disenfranchised and yada, yada, nada, *nicht und nacht*. Politics! He couldn't understand how people managed to take that crap seriously in their afterlife. Except for the fact that there was nothing else to do.

The doorbell rang. Mi do re sol. Sol re mi do. Except that, as one might expect in hell, the do was flat. Phil put down the phone and went to the front door, where there was a matched pair of blond teenage Satanists in tie-dyed caftans, like a salt-and-pepper set. He listened to their spiel for a while (even back in the real world he'd never been able to resist the grotty pathos of Jehovah's Witnesses) and looked at the tattoos on the girl's buttocks while the boy explained their diabolical significance. Phil waited till the girl, with her caftan down about her ankles again, started in on the deferred payment system that would let him enjoy the privileges of an Initiate of the Mystic Dawn without further waiting. Then *he* explained that he was penniless and only had a roof over his head through the good graces of his wife, the poet and filmmaker Joycelin Shrager, who was not a Satanist, although she did consult the *I Ching* from time to time. The Satanists looked disappointed but not surprised. They probably didn't get many takers, for this was not a prosperous part of hell. Farther south toward Acherontine Canyon was where you found the gangs and Republicans and people with money to burn.

He did think to ask, before the Satanists headed on to the neighbors, whether they had a joint they could spare or possibly some bennies. The girl obliged with a couple of Red Devils wrapped in a twist of foil.

At such moments Phil realized that there was a Higher Power in charge of his life, even here in hell. Also there was a certain kind of chick whose karmic doom was to be a doormat to his kind of sleazeball. One look and you could hear the orchestra tuning up for *Tristan*.

He swallowed the pills at once, not wanting to deal with Joycelin's passion for distributive justice (*mi casa es Sue's casa*). When they stuck halfway down, he had to find something to flush them down the rest of the way, which turned out to be the residue in a bottle of mescal, which he had no memory of having opened, or emptied.

Passing the kitchen door, he called out, "So, who's winning?"

Joycelin answered, "Bush. Which is tragic."

Phil felt a distinct chill of *déjà vu*, as though he'd lived through a Bush presidency once already here in hell. Would he now have to do it all over again? That seemed to be one of hell's basic ideas, Eternal Recurrence: Sisyphus pushing his rock up the mountain. The chicken crossing the road. The same Centrum ad over and over and over. It was tiresome, really, more than tragic, but for Joycelin any disappointment or delay was a tragedy. She had a very low tolerance for pain, which was how she'd risen so high so soon in hell's bureaucracy of minor demons, to the point where she had been given her pick among the newly damned for spouses. From having been, by her own declaration, his number one fan, she was now his main squeeze and even, if marriages made in hell were legal, his wedded wife.

Not that he wasn't grateful. He'd never been able to get through a day without the support system provided by matrimony. Joyce-lin might be shrewish, stupid, obese, piggishly selfish, and lazy but she *was* a wife, and that's what Phil needed for all those little domestic details he couldn't take care of himself if he wanted to get any writing done. The fact that he hadn't got any writing done for a while — not a single word put to paper since his fatal stroke and the move to the Styx! — was irrelevant. Phil *loved* Joycelin as much as he'd loved any of his wives in the real world, besides which she could always be counted on for a quick fuck (though never a blow job), and if sex with Joycelin was the rough equiva-lent of Alpo for dinner, well, you can learn to like Alpo.

Joycelin, with the wonderful telepathy peculiar to succubi, called out to him from the kitchen. "There's nothing in the cup-board but Alpo. Why don't you go to the Cathedral?"

"Why don't you?" he replied in a patient tone.

"Because I'm on the suicide hotline."

"Again?"

"I'm always on the hotline on Wednesdays. You know that."

"But it's always Wednesday!"

"Never mind. Eat the Alpo, I don't care."

So he was off to the First National Cathedral of Hell, thirty minutes along the Kurt Cobain Expressway, then along South Milton until the immense, smog-wrapped stainless steel spire loomed into view. Talk about your sense of wonder. Big? Hell held nothing grander or gaudier or more garish. It was a replica of the Crystal Cathedral that Philip Johnson had built for the televangelist Dr. Robert H. Schuller at the start of the Reagan era. Phil had visited the original edifice shortly before his stroke to witness its Christmas spectacular and fallen in love with its NASA-like glitz and bluster. It was the Cadillac Eldorado of cathedrals, and Phil's defibrillated heart had lit up when he discovered that there was a replica of it in his own neighborhood in hell.

Of course, it wasn't a Christian church any longer. As the Hagia Sophia had become an Ottoman mosque after the fall of Byzantium, so Dr. Schuller's monument had been converted to the worship of Satan. But what else would you expect in the infernal realm? Phil, who had always been of an ecumenical disposition, had no difficulty accepting a Satanic liturgy — as long as the musical component of the service was up to snuff, and in that regard he had no complaints. As no less an authority than Milton has noted of musical performances in the netherworld: "The harmony suspended hell, and took with ravishment the thronging audience."[22]

Attendance at First National offered a further benefit for those who would agree to register as Satanists and accept the mark of

---

22 *Paradise Lost* by John Milton, Book 11, 551–54.

Cain on their brows, and that was access to the cathedral's food kitchen. True, the shelves offered but a meager selection, and that limited to the staples customarily found in charity food-cupboards: canned sardines and artichoke hearts, pudding powders, strangely shaped pasta, and great pyramids of cans that had lost their labels and which usually turned out to be pet food. But protein is protein, and beggars can't be choosers. Not to mention, no sauce like appetite.

Phil took his place at the end of the waiting line for the food kitchen that was as long as any at Disneyland. There was a less dense parallel line of beggars and buskers trying to bully money from the people waiting for a handout. There were the usual multiply-pierced punks and punkettes, an inept juggler, a transvestite lip-synching to Callas's Norma's "*Casta diva*," entrancing even on a scratchy tape, and then the oddest old duffer with Andy Warhol glasses and a pixilated smile, who was handing out leaflets advertising the cathedral's amusement park.

"Aren't you Philip K. Dick?" the fellow asked, with a squint of his magnified eyes.

Phil beamed with pleasure, for it was unusual for him to be recognized by anyone in hell. "Why yes, I am!"

The man held out his hand, liver-spotted and knob-knuckled from arthritis. "How wonderful. *I'm* Philip Johnson, and I've been looking all over for you!"

Phil felt a shiver of uncleanliness as the man's fingers slipped round his own, as though he'd touched an animal of a tabooed totem. What was it about his handshake that was so...dismaying? Not the lack of any responsive pressure, not the softness of the flesh. What?

The warmth.

"You're alive," Phil marveled quietly.

"Oh," said the old man, with a twinkle of flirtatiousness, "you noticed. How nice of you. Yes, a ruin so to speak, very antique, but still my breath would cloud a mirror, and still my heirs live in fear. Yet, though living, I am able, like fabled Orpheus, to visit Dis. As the architect of the cathedral I have a special dispensation. And then too —" he brushed aside the bangs of feathery white hair to reveal the Mark of Cain "— I am a servant of Satan, which brings certain membership privileges. And so, I see, are you!"

Phil blushed. It was always a bit embarrassing to be recognized, by the mark on his brow, as someone's fellow Satanist — especially when they seemed, like this one, to be gay. "Hey," said Phil, "that's great. Heil, Satan!"

"Actually, Phil — Oh my, it just dawned on me — we're both Phils. How about that! Anyhow, Phil *mon frère*, it's no accident that I should have come upon you just now, since I have been looking for you high and low. With this in mind." With his left hand he patted the back of Phil's, still trapped in his too-fervid grasp. "An offer that, as they say, can't be refused. But only because it's simply too wonderful to be believed. Can you guess?"

"Not marriage, I hope."

Johnson's eyes glinted, briefly, with a sincere malice. *He* might jest about his gender preferences, but those of lower rank might not precede him to the jest. "No-o-o, not that. You have a spouse already, I believe. While I…" He waved his hand airily (dropping Phil's to do so), as though to declare his butterfly freedom. "I am forever a bachelor."

The glint narrowed and became steadier, laserlike. "Let me ask you, Phil — (This may be a painful question, forgive me.) How is your *work* going these days?"

"My work?"

"Your writing, Phil. You were always such a fecund soul. So

many novels! uncounted stories! *reams* of paper! A very Niagara of a novelist. What are you up to now?"

Phil realized the man already knew the answer to his question, so there wouldn't be much point lying. He had no face to save. He looked down at the dull asphalt of the cathedral close. "I haven't written a word since I came here. As you probably know."

"No!" Johnson echoed. "You? Writer's block? That's hard to believe."

"Yeah, but there it is. I'm just a hollow shell."

"Well, which of us is not, in some respect? But wouldn't you *like* to write again? Another novel? A tetralogy? Wouldn't that make the time pass more pleasurably? Your life before hell was not, in most respects, significantly different in its daily aspects than it is now. Your domestic circumstances are much the same: the house, the wife, the diet, even the car. But none of that mattered, I gather, so long as you were at one with your Muse, so long as the words flowed in a steady stream, and the pages of your manuscript amassed beside your typewriter. What would you give, Phil, to enjoy that facility again? *And* not just the reawakened power, but guaranteed publication once the work was done. For I can arrange to have whatever you may produce here discovered by your executors. As you well know, your least utterance has become holy writ to legions of readers. A posthumous novel by Philip K. Dick might well make the *New York Times* Best-seller List. Wouldn't that be worth an eternity in hell?"

"I'm tempted," Phil admitted. "But there's just one problem. Here." He tapped his clavicle.

"Within, you mean? Erectile dysfunction? We can cure that now."

"I don't have *ideas* any more. I'm empty."

"As to that, Phil, all you need is a drop, a *droplet*, of living blood.

Which *I* (as you noted earlier) still possess. Do you doubt me? Then taste this."

The aged architect took a stiletto from his pocket, flicked it open, and deftly sliced open the pointy tip of his tongue. A bead of blood formed at the cut, which rolled onto the waiting knife blade like a trained flea.

Johnson extended the knife, with its little sacrament, for Phil to partake. The tip of his tongue still protruded from his thin lips, oozing slow droplets of blood.

The sight excited Phil's appetite, and he took the knife and ran his own tongue along the blade. The droplet exploded through his palate like a depth charge, like raw nuggets of artificial cheese flavor that you can sometimes find at the bottom of a bag of Cheetos. It was intensely, vilely delicious like the anchovy butter that Joycelin had made for him on his birthday, substituting lard for butter (for there is never butter to be had in hell). His eyes returned to the sources of his pleasure, the blood still flowing from Johnson's tongue.

They kissed.

When it was over, Phil had a whole new novel in his head. It was just like the old days. The initial searing bolt of lightning, and then the quick, inevitable exfoliation of the story. If A, then B, and so on all the way to an end that would be tragical, comical, lyrical, and epistemologically devastating.

And the whole splendid tale would follow inexorably from the title: *Dick's Divine Comedy!* It amazed Phil that he hadn't written it already, since it slotted so perfectly into his existing *oeuvre*. It was the book he'd been born to write — and died, as well.

"Feeling inspired?" Johnson asked, wiping his sliced tongue with a silk hanky.

"Orpheus never felt more so," Phil assured him. After their kiss the old geezer probably thought Phil was as big a perv as he was, but that was okay with Phil. He would have sucked cock for a week in Alcatraz in order to feel like this again. He was juiced. High! Alive! God-damn, he'd forgotten what that was like. His whole being was the string on a violin and Menuhin was playing him and he was fucking *vibrating!* Whoopsy-doo!

"I'm glad that *you're* glad," said Johnson, tucking his hanky back in his breast pocket. "But there will be a price to pay, you know."

"Hey, tell me how much, and I'll pay it."

"But you must pay it *before* you write your new book."

"Yeah. Whenever. Sure."

Already he could feel the coil unwinding within him, the tension lessening, the brightness fading. But he could still envision the cover of the unwritten book: his own soulful face in a golden glow, eyes glinting as though he were sitting before a fire. And, in black gothic letters on a field of gilt, just as on the cover of Ciardi's Mentor Classic: *Dick's Divine Comedy.*

"Phil, are you listening?"

He nodded his head, fearful that to speak a word would make the vision fade faster.

"There is someone you will have to kill."

"Uh-huh." He nodded again.

"It's someone you've always wanted to kill, actually. An enemy. A critic. One who has written disrespectfully of your work, pretending to praise it but all the while hedging his words to make you seem the lesser writer. *And* he's a fag."

"Tom Disch?"

"Well, that's *almost* a bulls-eye."

"I can't think of anyone I'd rather kill. But won't it be a little difficult? I'm dead. And I take it he's still alive."

"He is, and so at the moment outside the range of your malice.

Disch is not the actual target. You might say that he's the target once removed. Your mission will be to kill his father. And to that end you'll have to travel back in time to the moment he was conceived. That is a trip *I* could never make, even with all hell helping. But you, being dead and a resident of Eternity, can do that. You'll find a wormhole back to 1939. Your destined victim, it will interest you to know, is a European author of considerable celebrity; a Nobelist, in fact."

"I thought you said I was going to kill Disch's father."

"And so you will, with Satan's help. At the same time you will change the course of World War II, just as in your Hugo Award-winning novel, *The Man in the High Castle*."

"Yeah, but in reverse. In my book it's the Nazis and the Japs who won the war."

"Yes, and the Nazis send over a hit man to kill the Swedish author of *The Grasshopper Lies Heavy*, a novel in which the U.S. has won the war. Which turns out, by the end of the book, to be the case. So we'll simply reverse that plot. You'll kill Thomas Mann —"

"Thomas Mann! No shit?"

Johnson nodded. "Mm-hm. That's who Disch's father was. Amazing, isn't it? But you'll soon see how that happened, or would have, as you'll have a ringside seat at the Leamington Hotel for the blessed event. Or non-event, since you'll be on hand to kill *both* his parents."

"I'm having difficulty believing this," said Phil.

"Oh, you've written stories a good deal more improbable than this. And you will again, once you've done this one job. But let me finish explaining: you'll kill Thomas Mann, and that will change the course of World War II (exactly how is another long story), *and* you will prevent the birth — nay, the very existence — of Thomas M. Disch —"

"And good riddance. You know, I tried, back in '74, to *warn* the FBI about him. I wrote them, off my own bat, after I'd read his book *Camp Concentration*, and I told them he was a probable subversive. And an *atheist!*"

"I know that, Phil. I've read your files. Indeed, they are now public knowledge, thanks to your biographer and the Freedom of Information Act. Your zeal in volunteering your services to the Bureau is one of the primary reasons you were sent to hell, as well as why the Bureau has chosen you to accomplish this very *sensitive* mission." Johnson emphasized his last phrase with a snake-ish flicker of his tongue.

Phil lusted for more of Johnson's living blood. Blood is like crack. Once you've had it, you never lose your craving for another taste. And another. And still more.

Chapter Nine

MONOTHEISM has a bad track record regarding diversity. Even American monotheists, though they give lip service to the notion that other people might have ideas of their own, are liable to brand other gods even slightly different from those they adore as liberal or otherwise not to be condoned. This was made painfully clear last night in a PBS documentary on the President's evangelical faith, which is scary in just the way the worshippers are at the Noah's Ark Pentecostal Mission and Children's Zoo in Chapter Six. Perhaps President Bush read that story when it first saw print in 1983.

I jest, of course. Monotheists don't need to read any book beyond the screed of their creed. Among Muslims it's the *Koran*, in Texas the *Holy Bible* (King James version), and those in A.A. read the Big Book, as they style it. True believers don't just read their holy writs, of course, they memorize them so that when they want to cinch an argument they can cite chapter and verse, and then, automatically, win. Henry Morris explains how that works in his treatise, *Scientific Creationism* (Master Books, 1985): "It is precisely because Biblical revelation is absolutely authoritative and perspicuous that the scientific facts, rightly interpreted, will give the same testimony as that of Scripture. There is not the slightest possibility that the *facts* of science can contradict the Bible."

How reassuring that is, especially if one doesn't want to be put to the bother of reading a lot of tedious textbooks about soil erosion and carbon dating and pterodactyls. That — reassurance, solace, balm — is what any holy writ is designed to provide. Poetry has much the same mission and makes the same promise ("That's all you know and all you need to know," Keats assures us after he's made one very dubious proposition in "Endymion"), but too often poetry lacks the guts to take the battle into the enemy camp. There have been a few rowdies like Alexander Pope and Kenneth Koch with a take-no-hostages attitude, but on the whole the arts are polytheist territory. There are, after all, *seven* muses.

A good bit of the holy writ I grew up with is given over to berating false gods and those who worship them. Idolatry was a big problem in olden days, from the Golden Calf that Moses had to contend with down to the Babylonian captivity when King Cyrus tried to get the prophet Daniel to worship Ba'al. By way of assuring Daniel that Ba'al was a living god the king pointed out what a huge appetite the god had. Every night when he was locked inside his temple Ba'al downed a whole banquet table of food and wine. Daniel, a proto-private eye, sprinkled the sealed banquet hall with dust, and next morning he showed Cyrus the footprints that the seventy priests of Ba'al along with their wives and children had left around the table as they were gobbling down the "living god's" dinner. Cyrus was furious and, to quote verse 22: "The king killed them [the seventy priests, their wives, and kids], and he turned Ba'al over to Daniel, who destroyed him and his temple."[23]

---

23 How timeless these Bible stories are, and how they keep recurring throughout history. Isn't this story of Daniel and the priest of Ba'al just Santa Claus in a different costume? What is always the most potent proof that Santa had been in the house? The fact that the cookies and milk that had

Elsewhere in the Apocrypha there is a rant against the pretensions of false gods, the "Letter of Jeremiah," a kind of *Atheism for Dummies*, in which the author draws up a long list of the insufficiencies of gods who are only silver, gold, and wood: they can't "set up a king, or put one down"; they can't give you money, or prevent death, or save weaklings from the strong; they can't make the blind see, or help widows and orphans. In sum: "These things made of wood and plated with gold or silver are like stones from the mountain, and those who attend them will be put to shame. Why then should anyone think them gods, or call them so?"[24]

These are dangerous thoughts to set before believers, for the faults that can be charged against false gods can often quite as easily be laid at Jehovah's door. Many a blind man has continued in his blindness despite the sacrifice of whole cotes of doves, and to this day there are widows and orphans (especially along the coastlines hit by the Christmas tsunami) for whom the God of Abraham and of Isaac has done squat. It may be that it is just such failures to deliver on the part of the god they've prayed to that provoke the faithful to their most bitter fulminations against Ba'al and other false gods. Psychologists have a term for that psychic mechanism.

The most fervent believers have always been the fiercest in their denunciations of those who believe otherwise than themselves. Witness Sir Walter Scott's magnificent old zealot of a madwoman, Mause, who, feeble as she is, storms against the King's redcoats so: "I will take up my testimony against you ance and again. — Philistines ye are, and Edomites — leopards are ye, and foxes — evening wolves, that gnaw not the bones till the morrow — wicked dogs

<hr>

been left out for him have disappeared.

24 From The Book of Baruch, 6:30–40, in *The Apocrypha, an American Translation* by Edgar J. Goodspeed (Vintage, 1938).

that compass about the chosen — thrusting kine and pushing bulls of Bashan — piercing serpents ye are, and allied baith in name and nature with the great Red Dragon; Revelations, twelfth chapter, third and fourth verses."[25]

An uninvolved onlooker at such moments may be inclined to think Mause's wrath burns as bright in proportion as it is impotent, that those whose gods are firmly impedestaled can better afford some show of tolerance. President Bush, for instance, is notable for his quiet smirk whenever he deflects a question about his religious faith. Such silence speaks volumes. It's only losers who make a fuss and only hopeless losers who fly off the handle like mad old Mause. Even so, we should not overlook the possibility that those of a cantankerous or bilious temperament will gravitate to lost causes by way of keeping their furnace stoked. Hatred can pre-exist its objects.

But we've strayed far afield from what I meant to be the focus of this chapter, the comfort-food aspect of holy writ, the way a little wisdom can act as an antidote to all life's slings and arrows. As it does it the following small sheaf of Scriptures[26]:

Proverbs

1. There is a man weeping as he sits by a roulette table, in Atlantic City: he has lost everything, he is ruined.
2. Another weeps as, yet again, the mailman drives by without stopping.
3. In a suburb outside Middletown tears of despair moisten a long-unlaundered pillowcase at 3 A.M.

---

25 *Old Mortality* by Sir Walter Scott, Chapter 8 (Ticknor and Fields, 1857).
26 from the *Hudson Review*, Summer 1998.

4. These men are fortune's fools who baselessly believed luck would favor them always because they had been lucky once.

5. They shall turn to their comforters and find no comfort. Their dinners are take-out, their wives live in distant cities.

6. I say to them: stop bellyaching. Mow your lawns. Rejoice in the music of Beethoven, and brush your teeth.

7. Behold a procession of women approaches. They are old but their faces are bright with makeup. They do not complain of arthritis or their children's neglect.

8. Here is a widow who paints landscapes and clowns. How chipper she is, how full of wisdom.

9. Here is her sister Judith. Four hours every day she speaks with strangers on the phone about their asphalt driveways, and never repines.

10. This woman's house is spotless. She breakfasts on her own preserves. Her hands are always busy.

11. How long the days are in July, how much there is still to be done.

12. Do not grieve, therefore, for resorts that stand empty in the Catskills, where once were multitudes; nor for the rivers where no bass strike; nor yet for the small town's only five-and-dime, burned to the ground.

13. What though there is not money for a wider drive: do not, each spring, the irises return?

14. The deer and the crow delight beneath the apple tree; the wise man sits by his TV and drowses, and the mouse is warm in the crawlspace.

15. Why, therefore, sorrow? A millennium draws to
    an end, but shall not another replace it?

16. Look on this book, a best-seller long ago, and just
    today purchased for two dollars at the Methodists'
    Book Bazaar.

17. There is no death but only continuance; if not for
    those who have passed away, at least for all the
    rest of us.

18. The nonagenarian in the nursing home has heard the
    Nightly News, but her sleep is undisturbed.

19. The downsized trucker drinks his fill, and the chroni-
    cally depressed waitress grows fat.

20. Above them all are the stars, beyond summary or com-
    prehension; beyond all sorrow equally: unthinkable
    their distance from us.

21. And yet, how wonderful to think, it is those stars,
    so far away, that are the source of all our luck.

22. Let the wise heed these counsels, and let the ignorant
    live in their ignorance still. Selah.

Chapter Ten

I CAN'T BELIEVE we're already at Chapter Ten. It was only Christmas Eve when Chapter One got launched, and today is the Epiphany. Speaking of which I have just had one of my own. All along I've been fretting whether *Why I Am God*, the title I've been working with (and that got my juices flowing), might be a curse from a publisher's point of view. He might take one look and think, "Who does he think he's kidding?" or even, "Christ, another Salman Rushdie!" And for all I know he might be right. Some zealot with no one else better to kill might revenge his god's honor (and get his own picture in the papers) by going after the perpetrator of any book called *Why I Am God*.

So, instead, how about *The Word of God* while keeping the old subtitle, *Holy Writ Rewritten*. That way potential jihadis would have to actually open the book and start reading (something jihadis aren't likely to do) before they could be sure I was an instrument of Satan. If that sounds craven, so be it. Gods like me take a lofty view of human weakness and can ignore name-calling. I doubt that Ba'al so much as blinked when Jeremiah's letter in the Apocrypha as quoted above first appeared in print, and Santa Claus, when he's accused of not existing, can simply point to that old journalistic standby, "Yes, Virginia, there *is* a Santa Claus!" Nuff said.

So, the old title goes, but not the first four-word paragraph. Stet *Let there be light!* Though I will take this revisionary opportunity to point out that there is an unspoken assumption in those divine words — to wit, that light has its own propensity for existing and only needs God's nod of permission to start shining. It's like "Let my people go," or "Let them eat cake," but without the sarcasm that Marie Antoinette probably intended. It's conceivable that light might have come into being all on its own, without my having let it, which is pretty much what the Big Bang theory of cosmology supposes. Time out of mind we gods have known that light will be, whether we liked it or not. As our mothers used to say, *Che sara, sara.*

In my youth I thought I was a real whiz at math, and I was good enough to land a job as a structural steel draftsman right after I graduated high school, but later in college I met my mathematical Waterloo in integral calculus. No longer did each new page of the textbook offer its *Eureka!* moment. And that's how it is that in these pages I must simply refer you to the established authorities for a fuller accounting of all cosmological wisdom. You can read Carl Sagan or Stephen Hawking, or get a degree in astrophysics, or (if you're lazy like me) just look up at the heavens on some clear night in January and marvel. (But wear something warm.)

Such advice may strike younger, intellectually restless readers as unadventurous and time-serving. They'd like a cosmology that can offend the know-it-all grown-ups who tell them the Earth is round and that they shouldn't smoke or drive while drinking alcohol. You can take your universe and shove it! My two Mormons in Amecameca rampaged against Darwin not so much from intellectual conviction but because he could be counted on as a *casus belli*: "Say 'Evolution' again and I'll cream ya!" And who's going to stand up for Darwin but the nerds and wimps who will be emigrating to Harvard and MIT after graduation instead of enlisting in the Marines?

Like the clothes we wear and the restaurants we eat at, the gods we worship are a declaration of our social class. In our younger years we may not be aware of the rift that separates Episcopalian from Methodist, or the gulf between both sects and those who attend *Nuestra Señora de Guadalupe*, and the real abyss between all those and the Taliban at the other end of the Earth. School-marms still inculcate a universal and undiscrimating benevolence toward those who are diverse, and not till he or she is flown off to the battlefields of the Middle East does the average young American realize that there are whole countries and religions that hate his guts and his gods.

Tomorrow, for instance, the Saudi cleric Aed Al-Qarni will advise worshippers at his mosque: "Throats must be slit and skulls must be shattered. This is the path to victory... The most people do today is to verbally protest over the TV channels or to demonstrate. What is the use of this? We must sacrifice people like Abd Al-Aziz Al-Rantisis and Ahmad Yassin, and thousands of others. Houses and young men must be sacrificed. If the idolatrous people of Vietnam, Cambodia, and South Africa, nations with no calling or divine law, can sacrifice people, blood, and souls, all the more reason we of the nation of Islam should do so."[27]

Another Saudi religious personage, Muhammad Al-Munajiid, has his own Islamic solution to the ever-perplexing problem of evil. The Christmas tsunami has disturbed the faith of many in the Islamic world, as once the Lisbon earthquake unsettled the faith of Catholics, since it appeared that most victims were co-religionists. However, the Saudi cleric revealed that the tsunami

---

27 Confirmation of this prophecy can be found in an article by Arnaud de Borchgrave in the *Washington Times* of Jan. 10, 2005.

was actually directed against Christians as a punishment for "the Christian holidays that are accompanied by forbidden things, by immorality, abomination, adultery, alcohol, drunken dancing, and revelry. A belly dancer costs 2,500 pounds a minute and a singer costs 50,000 pounds an hour, and they hop from one hotel to another from night to dawn." Little wonder Allah had to step in and do something! If that belly dancer is still hopping about from hotel to hotel, undeterred by the tsunami, a meteor could be next!

However, the tsunami may not be Allah's will at all. M. Vilmot, a Sri Lankan baker and a Buddhist, believes that he and fourteen members of his family were spared by the tsunami because they follow the five principles of Theravada Buddhism and don't lie, steal, drink, philander, or eat meat. Many other Sri Lankan Buddhists concurred, though they expressed bewilderment at why God would kill their own innocent children along with meat-eating Christians. Perhaps the tsunami was a collaborative effort between Allah and the Buddhists' god, and the two gods were obliged to allow a certain number of the other's worshippers to die as a trade-off for his own vengeance.

I jest, which is a god's prerogative. That is probably the best way to deal with the problem of evil, if one is a god. To claim responsibility for every tsunami that comes along won't get us anywhere. Just read the Book of Job, where God answers Job's rants with his own unbecoming brags about how big he is, how powerful, how above and beyond reproach. And why? Because he says so! As Virginia Woolf commented in her journal: "I read the Book of Job last night — I don't think God comes well out of it."

Too true. That's why this god doesn't claim responsibility for the tsunami of a month ago, or the Lisbon earthquake, or boils and rashes on whomever they may be visited. The problem of evil isn't *my* problem. When I deal out justice, it's poetic justice, like Dante's. The wages of sin are neither death nor 2,500 pounds a minute (which comes out to over a million pounds for one eight-hour shift!); the wages of sin are usually less than the minimum wage — and even so there are sinners.

There have been entire long books written about the problem of evil, but this won't be one of them. Situational ethics supposes that there are as many problems of evil as there are evildoers creating the problem. As to tsunamis, what can I say? Shit happens.

Chapter Eleven

IN THE REALM OF ETHICS, evil will continue to be a problem as long as there are evildoers. It is in regard to tsunamis and other so-called "acts of God" that I disclaim any personal responsibility for the problem of evil. No god, however, can evade the related problem[28] posed by death. People want to be told they're not going to die, and they want to extend that exemption to their friends and relatives. When a child says his prayers at night, he calls on God to bless his mommy and daddy, etc. Prayerwise such a Guardian Life policy is every believer's daily minimum requirement. When Voltaire quipped that if God didn't exist we would have to invent him, he probably had that life-insurance aspect of God particularly in mind.

Tsunamis happen in another hemisphere, and earthquakes are peculiar to Lisbon and San Francisco, but Death is everywhere. He (or she) lurks in alleyways, slicks winter roads with ice, haunts hospital waiting rooms, and carouses in taverns into the wee hours. I speak here not of the death in an astronomical sense — death equated with the stilly night of outer space, who was invoked in my poem about the moon — but of Death as a personage whom

---

28 Related most intimately in Milton's cosmology, where they form a mother/son duo, Sin having brought Death into the world. As ever, a woman takes the fall.

we are all destined to encounter in the days to come. As to his (or her) sex we can't be a sure: a skeleton is gender-neutral. The death gods of Greece and Rome and of the Aztecs were male, and I've usually assumed that the Death of Gothic portals and medieval ballad sheets is a guy, as well. He is in Ingmar Bergman's *The Seventh Seal* and in my own story, "Death and the Single Girl,"[29] although in that story he suffers erectile dysfunction and is consequently unable to hold up his end of the "I come/you go" contract. But there have been some fine female death-bringers. In *Die Walküre* Brünhilde appears to Siegmund in the solemnly creepy *Todesverkundigung* scene announcing his imminent death in battle; the Japanese kabuki theater offers similar moments.

But the greatest female avatar of death is Kali, aka Bhowanee, destroyer goddess of Hinduism and patron deity of the Thuggees, a sect of divinely sanctioned murderers active from the 14th through the 19th centuries. Kali, at the dawn of time, had fought a demon, whose every drop of blood shed in their battle yielded a new demon. Kali retaliated by creating from her own sweat two disciples who killed these enemy demons by strangulation, thus drying up the supply of blood-born demons. Kali's disciples and their posterity were thereafter licensed to go on strangling human victims and pocketing the profits.[30]

I must say that I find such behavior in a god or in her worshipers reprehensible. Kali seems no better to me than Charlie Manson. Indeed, I have more respect for your average street-corner rapist and killer than for a goddess who turns her worship into a branch of Murder, Inc. For shame, Kali, for shame! And the same strictures apply to Allah when he organizes his worshippers in

29 "Death and the Single Girl," *Getting into Death* (Knopf, 1976).
30 For a vivid account of Kali and her Thuggees' collision with the British Empire, I recommend Captain Meadows Taylor's 1839 best-seller, *Confessions of a Thug* (Stein and Day, 1968).

Afghanistan and elsewhere in profit-oriented criminal conspira-
cies. (The age-old connection between drug use and religious fer-
vor is a complex and vexed issue, and will be dealt with in a chapter of its own.)

The Aztec god of death (forgive me but I cannot spell his name)
was no nicer than Kali. Like her he favored an extremely punk style
of self-adornment, heaping himself and his priests with skulls,
viscera, and flayed skins. No chthonic god can entirely escape a
Halloweenish first impression, but usually he sweetens it with the
equivalent of candy. Like the Commendatore in *Don Giovanni*, he
observes the decorums of a civilized life. If his handshake seems
overdone, even crushing, well, nobody's perfect.

All this as preamble to a poem of my own about Death — no,
two poems — written decades ago, as a propitiation and a sport.

How to Behave When Dead[31]

A notorious tease, he may pretend
not to be aware of you.
Just wait.
He must speak first. Then
you may begin to praise him.

Remember:
sincerity and naturalness
count for more than wit.
His jokes may strike you as
abstruse.
Only laugh if he does.

---

31 ABCDEFG HIJKLM NPOQRST UVWXYZ (Anvil Press, 1981).

Gifts?
They say he's mad for art,
but whether in the melting
elegaic mode of say, this
Vase of Poppies
or, turning the mirror
to his own face, a bronze skull
gorging on a snake —
that is a matter of taste.
In any case, the expense
is what he notices.

What to wear.
Some authorities
still insist on black.
But really, in this modern age,
your best is all that is required.

Come, Pleasant Death[32]

Come, pleasant Death, and decorate my tomb
With lush, banal decalcomania!
Sink me as you sank the Lusitania!
Enshroud me with your deep Miltonic gloom!
Come, dressed in leather, blacker than the night
The power failed and all the lights went out.
Come, ravish me, and let me no more doubt
Your boots can trample and your teeth can bite!

---

32 from *Orders of the Retina* (Toothpaste Press, 1982).

— *Like this! Your belly slack and tattoos dim!*
Your arches fallen and a double chin?
A plastic handle on your riding crop?
When was the last time you were at a gym?
I really wonder that they let you in.
Dear Death, do let's just let the matter drop.

As I looked through old books and sheaves for those two spec-imens I realized that I could put together rather a large volume devoted entirely to elegies and tributes to Death in his various guises. Thus, from just the last few years, there have been full-scale funerary odes for Kenneth Koch, Derrida, and Princess Di (the last in the manner of William McGonagall), and a short lyric written "On the Bus to A. R. Ammons's Memorial Service." In younger years I beat Death to the punch a couple of times by writ-ing elegies for people before they were actually deceased (my old friend John Sladek and the poet Amy Clampitt), in much the way that newspapers have obits written against the day that they'll be needed. "The Art of Dying," which Richard Howard took for *New American Review*, invented more interesting deaths for a whole catalogue of famous poets. I did a poem defending the aesthet-ics of Forest Lawn (the California cemetery that Evelyn Waugh demolished in *The Loved One*), an ill-tempered anti-Nixon gibe, "At the Tomb of the Unknown President," and a very pretty lyric called "The Decaying Swan," written as a class assignment for David Lehman (I was a visitor; too old, alas, to have been his stu-dent), which was to "translate" a poem from a language we didn't understand.

Et cetera, et cetera. I have been *more* than half in love with ease-ful Death, and he has so far rewarded my devotion with a policy of benign neglect. Across the years he has shown the same kindness to many of his poetic courtiers and sycophants. Tennyson, who wrote such first-rate elegies as "In Memoriam" and "Ode on the Death of the Duke of Wellington,"[33] lived to a ripe old age, and even John ("Death, thou art dead") Donne, for all his taunts, made it to fifty-nine.

When I began this chapter I'd entirely forgotten the poem with which it must inevitably be rounded off, since it not only ties a tidy bow on the package but serves as a good segué to Chapter 12: an elegy for one of the characters here, Philip K. Dick, written on Easter Sunday, 1982, shortly after Dick's death at the unripe middle age of fifty-four.

Ode on the Death of Philip K. Dick[34]

God, if there is a God, and that is something
He could never decide, has thrown him away.
A dumb thing to do, you say? With so much juice
Still to be squeezed, with all that doom could do
To force new bloom from the pollardings
Of late middle age? He might have suffered much more.
Or he might, let us admit it, have got himself
A golden tan under the sunlamps of success,
Written his memoirs, and made friends with Leviathan.

This way he dies unreconciled, and we are left
With his books buzzing on our stained-pine shelves,
Their sting and sweetness frozen by the flashcube

---

33 A poem from which I pried loose the title for my early novel *Echo Round His Bones* (Berkley, 1967).

34 *Here I Am, There You Are, Where Were We* (Hutchinson, 1984), first appeared in *Washington Post Book World*, 1982.

Of his timely exit. Finis, he wrote, then wadded
Up the paper and swallowed it — though literally
That is exactly what he did not do. A suicide
Only by omission: he forgot to take the pill
His heart required, informing God, if He exists,
That He would have to keep it ticking by Himself.

I scarcely knew the man and have no right
To trim his obsequys with my romances.
There will be flowers from the studio that did
Its level best to level his best book
(But with, it should be understood, his blessing);
A special wreath, perhaps, from Harrison Ford,
Who (I'm told) he thought had meant to murder him:
Hollywood's latest, greatest star his murderer!
Lord, he had no need of my romancings!

And yet I'm sure he would have wanted them,
For he loved, as much as any 5-year-old, to hear
His story told — how little Philip all alone
Set off along the darkling road and won the love
Of Linda Ronstadt, or would have if she'd known
Him as we knew him, who loved him and still do,
Though only in the useless way we love
The newly dead. No, don't fret. Your story
Isn't over. We won't turn the lights off, yet.

What other things did Philip do? Were there
Giants that he slew? Dungeons where in chains
He languished? Were there witches and enchanters?
Did he dance on California's golden lawns?

Did his words assault the mighty, like the words
Of John the Baptist in Strauss's Salome?
There were. He did. But his words of prophecy,
Alas, were drowned by braying brasses,
Unheard by all our Herods and Herodiases.

Yet, as every poet knows, melodies are
Sweeter so. They are the honey ravens bring
To feast the poet in the desert of his heart —
Might-have-beens, imaginings, false starts.
For a while their wings will hover overhead;
Then, still unperceived, depart. Art,
In a word: art as the uniter of lobe
To love, of sic to non, of hick to city
Slicker; art as our reason for being writers.

Well, Philip, have I said it yet? The bitter,
Insufficient truth? I love you. It's not a love
To ease your feet from the concrete shoes
Of your completed oeuvre, nor yet a love
To warm your flesh or even earn you
Royalties. But let me say, for all your fans,
I love you, and I know that you'll return,
Our divo redivivus, *each time your voice*
Is summoned from the earth to tell its tale.

Chapter Twelve

The School for Traitors

"ALTHOUGH WE KNOW that this is not Dante's hell," the lecturer said, peering out over the rims of her reading glasses, "yet tradition exercises an undeniable authority over the individual imagination. It is so that we each inhabit the hell of our own making, but we buy our hells off the rack, as it were. For we who are damned Dante is as inescapable as Marks and Spencer, or should I say, for those among us who haven't shopped in London, the Gap? No one has yet come up with a more considered hell than Dante's; a juster hell; or one more commodious, with room for everyone. Admittedly there are areas of behavior we today reprobate more sternly than did he; we sin in ways yet to be invented in Dante's day. For instance, he came up with no torment to showcase the evils of drug abuse. But on the whole his Inferno has a niche suited to almost any sin you can commit. Certainly he has a place for all of *you*, and indeed, here you are in it — your home in Antenora."

A twelve-year-old in the first row of the lecture hall raised his hand. "Could you spell 'Antenora,' please."

Miss West, smiling that constricted and sickly smile reserved for teachers' pets, spelled the word and explained, further, that it was derived from the name of the Trojan, Antenor, who was believed to have betrayed his city to the Greeks. "Antenora is quite ghastly, as we know. The weather is arctic, television reception is primitive, pets simply aren't safe, and there is no respect for the aged and infirm. But beneath Antenora there are still two levels of deeper perdition, Ptolomæa, which is reserved for those who betray the sacred bonds of hospitality —"

Someone snickered at the back of the hall.

"Mrs. Rosenberg, do you have something you want to share with the class?"

Everyone shifted round to look at Ethel Rosenberg,[35] who blushed in two ovals just where the electrodes had wired her to the electric chair. "I just hadn't imagined that hospitality was so…" she faltered. "I mean, what did they do? Serve someone a really cheap white wine?"

"No," said the older woman in a tone that conveyed that she was a Dame Commander of the British Empire who would never have drunk a drop of an inferior wine. "By and large, those in Dante's Ptolomæa would invite people into their homes and kill them. You're an American: think of Anthony Perkins in *Psycho*."

The twelve-year-old in the front row gave a snort of amusement. Before he could ask, Miss West spelled out Ptolemæa, which is tricky even for most grown-ups. Then she resumed her orientation lecture:

"At the very bottom, frozen solid, is Judecca, the heart of darkness, where one may find Brutus and Cassius and Judas, and, by the sound of it, all the Jews of the Diaspora, though Dante

---

35 Ethel Rosenberg, a Communist spy, electrocuted with her husband Julius, on June 19, 1953. The Rosenbergs' innocence became an article of faith among American liberals, especially as set forth in E. L. Doctorow's novel, *The Book of Daniel* (Random House, 1971), in which the innocence of his fictional traitors is somehow innate, the inverse of original sin.

doesn't spell that out. He didn't have to. Christians of his era simply assumed that all Jews, as traitors to Christ, would share the fate of Judas.

"It has been said that treason is not so much a sin as a vocation. Indeed, I was the one to say it, in my book, *The Meaning of Treason*, and in its revised and expanded version, *The New Meaning of Treason*, published in 1965, but alas no longer in print. In that book I demonstrate how the ultimate goals of Fascist spies in World War II were the same as those of Communist spies in the Cold War era. Both are the servants of death and enemies of democratic government, as *you* are all well aware. Yes, Mr. Hiss?"

Alger Hiss rose to his feet and brushed back a lock of his distinguished gray hair. In a well-modulated baritone he said, "Just for the record, Miss West, I should like to note that I have never been a Communist, much less a Communist spy."

There was a murmur of agreement among those assembled in the hall, each of whom, evidently, wanted to attest to an equal innocence.

"Duly noted," said Miss West. "Now, if I may continue…?"

Hiss sat. The murmurs abated.

"To resume: Treason, in our time, can be thought of as a vocation, like the priesthood, the piano, or the Mafia. Some teens are inspired to be the next Madonna, a new Paderewski, another John Gotti. Others long to be another Alger Hiss or Julius Rosenberg — Mr. Hiss, please sit, we have already registered your objection — to be, that is to say, wicked in some absolute and unequivocal way, to betray *everything* they believe in. They would commit treason against the land of their birth not because that land is evil, but because they are. Theirs are the proud despairs of Milton's Satan, who said (I quote from memory):

> *So, farewell hope, and with hope farewell fear,*
> *Farewell remorse: All good to me is lost;*
> *Evil, be thou my good*[36]

"All of you here have thrilled to those lines, as one might the first time one sees one's own name in print, whether as an author or a felon: there it is, in black and white, proof of the existence of God — the God of Self. But there are lines by Milton still more thrilling, and though I am sure you all know them by heart, allow me the pleasure of repeating them aloud:

> *Me miserable! which way shall I fly*
> *Infinite wrath, and infinite despair?*
> *Which way I fly is Hell; myself am Hell;*
> *And in the lowest deep, a lower deep*
> *Still threatening to devour me opens wide,*
> *To which the Hell I suffer seems a Heaven.*[37]

"The reason you are assembled here today is to be given a chance to share in that great Miltonic promise, to sink into that lower deep, to be devoured by a further infernal abyss, to commit a treason blacker than your blackest treason heretofore.

"Are there any questions?"

Robert Hanssen raised his hand.

"Yes, Mr. Hanssen?"

"It's not about anything you said, or Milton either. I just wondered if you hadn't forgot something?"

"And what would that be, Mr. Hanssen?"

"Like starting off with a prayer? Where we would stand in a

---

36 Milton, *Paradise Lost*, Book iv.

37 Ibid. l. 73.

circle and join hands." There was another murmur and a nodding of heads and the entire assembly spontaneously regrouped themselves so as to link their hands in a continuous human rosary, each bead of which in sequence recited a single couplet of the Traitor's Creed, which they all had down by heart.

Hanssen[38] began:

> *Dear Lord, we swear to be untrue*
> *And false in every deed we do.*

Vidkun Quisling,[39] holding his left hand, continued:

> *Our puppy loves all lechery,*
> *Our wedding vow a treachery.*

Quisling's Norwegian-inflected baritone was followed by the accentless mid-American countertenor of Larry Wu-tai Chin[40]:

> *We ask thee with our dying breath:*
> *Vouchsafe dishonor before death.*

Last of all Mata Hari,[41] in a tea gown specially created by Liberty of London, declaimed:

---

38   Robert Philip Hanssen (born in 1944) joined the FBI in 1976 and began working for the Communists in 1979. A devout Catholic, Hanssen attended the church of St. Catherine of Siena in Richmond, Virginia, for weekly services with his wife and six children.

39   Vidkun Quisling (1887–1945) was raised to the position of "minister president" of the Nazi puppet government of Norway on February 1, 1942 — one day before the Author's second birthday.

40   Larry Wu-tai Chin, a CIA analyst, committed suicide in his jail cell in 1986, having been convicted of selling American secrets to the Chinese for over thirty years.

41   Mata Hari (1876–1917), the stage name of Margaretha Geertruida Zelle, the wife of a Dutch colonial officer, who claimed to have been a Javanese temple dancer. A spy for both the French and German intelligence offices, she was executed by the French.

A single rule's our Holy Writ:
To be a perfect hypocrite.

"Thank you," said Miss West, when the traitors had disengaged and sat down again. "That was egregious, and quite unnecessary. Now before someone suggests that we all stand on our heads to recite the Pledge of Allegiance —" She paused a moment to allow for this possibility. "— I should like to explain the literally epoch-making undertaking that the forces of evil have assigned to us — nothing less than to reverse the course of history. But first I think it would be useful to consider a theme that has been the subject of discourse in this very hall from the time of the earliest heretics, predestination and free will. To what degree are our sins our own, and to what degree are they due to forces beyond our control? Is the young rapist who obeys a voice, which only he can hear, telling him to enter the bedroom of a woman he does not know and forcibly to sodomize and then strangle her, responsible for that act? Assuming, always, that the purported voice is not an outright lie. Was he compelled to obey that voice? Are any of us compelled to obey the undeniably real voices that may tell us, for instance, to murder everyone in Rwanda who is not a Catholic, or all the Jews in Poland? In short, isn't there a reason for everything that happens, so that the whole universe is just one big logic problem, with *ifs* leading to thens in an endless chain of causation? And if it was our all-knowing Creator who set this big logic machine in motion, then how should *we* be held responsible who are only its cogs and levers?

"It follows, does it not, that *we are all innocent?* Even Iago, and Edmund in *Lear*, and Richard the Third and Lady Macbeth. 'Tomorrow and tomorrow and tomorrow,' as her husband has said, and 'tomorrow and tomorrow' one might add, *and* have the whole thing graven on Hellgate. It would be quite as apt as 'Abandon hope' and cheerier in its way. For isn't that also the theme of Little Orphan Annie: 'Tomorrow! Tomorrow!' So long as time stretches on and on, there is time to undo the mistakes we've made. Like Penelope we can unweave yesterday's tapestry and start afresh tomorrow. And if yesterday, why not the day before yesterday as well? And maybe the day before that!

"Surely, this is not unimaginable. What's done *can* be undone, especially here in hell, where undoing is our forte, together with every other negative and contrary. So this is what I would propose, the task that Satan sets us, is nothing less than to rewrite history so that Germany is the victor of World War II!"

"Yes!" The twelve-year-old in the front row leapt to his feet, spreading his arms in the v of triumphal delight traditional to sporting events around the world. "*Deutschland über Alles! Hurrah!*"

Miss West smiled a permissive smile. Such rowdiness was to be indulged, even encouraged in the young. "The idea excites you, Philip?" she asked the boy.

"Does it ever! I mean, could you ask for any bigger turnaround than *that*? Unless maybe if you stopped the asteroid from hitting the Earth that killed all the dinosaurs."

"Well, perhaps in some other parallel universe Satan may accomplish that feat as well. But I think that all of us here will agree with young Philip that one could scarcely aspire to a more daunting goal — one that might seem, at first glance, insurmountable. Yet while there are still living intelligences on the Earth who were alive at the crucial juncture, the *Zusammenklappbarzeit* (I hope I did not mispronounce that; my German isn't very good), then the possibility remains of reweaving history's tapestry, of undoing D-Day and snatching victory from the jaws of defeat."

"Yes!" said the boy. "Heil, Satan! Hallelujah! And you know what? It's *my* idea!"

"And so it is, Philip. So it is. Would you like to come up to the podium and explain to your classmates how you managed to do that, and you a lad of only twelve?"

The boy came to the dais and faced the assembly, which was drawn from nations, races, and creeds the world over. Of all the traitors there he was the youngest, a distinction that commanded their resentful envy and respect. Yet even knowing him to be a traitor it was hard to think the boy other than he seemed — a typical nerdy American brat of the lower-middle class, with a bad haircut, acne dotting his forehead, and a little hard-on visible through his khaki pants.[42]

"Hi," said the boy, "My name is Philip K. Dick, and though you wouldn't suppose it to see me now, I am a world-famous science fiction writer. My books have sold millions of copies, and several have been made into blockbuster movies. Arnold Schwarzenegger starred in one of them! Some of you may be thinking, that's not possible, he's still a kid. But I just *look* like a kid. Inside of this twelve-year-old all-American boy is a bitter, burnt-out, alcoholic all-American loser, which is a kind of reversal of the usual situation, though I shouldn't have to be the one to point that out. Anyhow, there's a good reason why I'm twelve again, and that's because in order to be a double agent in the real world you have to have had a real body of flesh and blood at the time you visit. That's how time travel works. Now in April of 1939, the year of the *Zusammenklappbarzeit* that Miss West was speaking of, I would have been twelve years old. Actually eleven, but I was always mature for my chronological age.[43] So when I return to that period I also return

---

42 It is to be understood that in hell everyone of the male sex has an erection at all times.

43 In fact, Dick was born on December 16, 1928, and would have been ten years old in April of 1939.

to the body I had then, which is this one. And you know what? It doesn't feel that different. You'd think you'd feel a whole lot better in the body you had when you were twelve, but I don't. Maybe it's part of being in hell, or maybe I should have been more athletic when I was a kid. Anyhow.

"The whole thing about Germany actually winning World War II? That is my idea: read *The Man in the High Castle*. Another idea that I had first was the Jim Carrey movie called *The Truman Show*, in which this guy is living in an artificial world that's been created just to deceive him, so he can be watched in this soap opera the whole world is watching. That's taken from *Time Out of Joint* and also partly from *The Penultimate Truth*. But I think the worst case of someone stealing my ideas was a book called *Camp Concentration*, which was completely my own idea, but this other writer, Disch, had the same agent that I did, and the agent must have shown him my outline, which I'd forgot all about. That's how I am, I have so many great ideas I just forget half of them. But when Disch took my idea, he turned it around, and he made it a Communist type of story. Talk about 'Look What They've Done to My Song'! Of course, when I read his book and realized what had happened I had no choice, I had to contact the FBI. It was a national security threat. Which is how I got to be friends with J. Edgar Hoover.[44] But that's another story. Anyhow.

"What goes around comes around, as they say, and now it's payback time for Disch. If we all do this right, we are going to be able to wipe the bastard clean out of existence *and*, just as a side benefit, we can help Hitler to have a second chance to win the war, just like in *The Man in the High Castle*. How will we do this? you

---

44   This is doubtful. Dick wrote to denounce Disch to the FBI in October, 1972. Hoover had died a few months earlier.

must be asking yourselves. By seeing to it that Disch was never born is how!

"Let me ask you all a question. How many people here in the hall have read *Death in Venice* by Thomas Mann? All of you! I'm not surprised, it's a classic of German literature. What it may surprise you to know (it did me) is that Tom Disch is actually the illegitimate son of Thomas Mann, the regrettable result of a one-night stand between Mann, who was touring the country for the State Department, and his mother, Helen, a raven-haired Scandinavian beauty, the daughter of Norwegian immigrant farmers. I needn't remind *you*, Vidkun Quisling, that Norway itself was at that time (we're talking 1939, 1940) in the shadow of the Axis powers. Yet though the swastika would soon fly over Oslo, Norway's merchant marine fleet, the fourth largest in the world, would desert its native fjords to sail with British convoys. Isn't *that* treason?"

A dutiful chorus of "Treason!" and "Traitors!" and "Shame!" sounded in the hall.

"A traitor, yes! Touring the country to deliver his diatribes against his homeland in every church basement and synagogue, with his son Klaus and his daughter Erica at his side, both of them known homosexuals! And worse, thought to be guilty of an incestuous love! Little wonder, I should say, with such a father.

"Oh, if only some patriot had dared to put an end to the life of Thomas Mann! If only that tongue had been silenced before it could spread more of its venom! Perhaps Roosevelt might not have so easily tricked the Americans into entering the war. In that case, surely, Britain would have fallen to the Axis forces, and Europe would have been a true fortress with the Atlantic for a moat.

"That is the vision of an alternate history I offer you. I have offered it to you once already, as *The Man in the High Castle*, and you gave me the Hugo Award as my reward. I offer it again as the first step toward a more thrilling and truly Satanic reality. Grapple it to your false hearts, my fellow traitors, and make this your battle cry:

"Death! Death and eternal darkness take the soul of Thomas Disch!"

Everyone in the vast hall rose to take up the chant of the frenzied child, while Miss West looked on with pride.

The boy was now possessed by his daemon, his eyeballs rolled back to show only their whites, foam frothing at his lips, the mark of Cain glowing brightly on his acned forehead. He spoke in a rapid gibberish of Hollywood German, all *Achtung!*s and *Gesundheit!*s, but spewed forth with such a passion of malice as to make him seem an infantine avatar of the great dictator himself. He flailed his arms, as though to grasp for some unseen weapon with which to gun down his classmates in seventh grade.

And all the while, as though it were *Furtwängler* at the podium, the crowd of traitors continued their chant of "Death! Death and eternal darkness take the soul of Thomas Disch!"

As suddenly as the spirit had possessed the child it departed. The mark of Cain faded from his brow, and he wiped the spittle from his lips. "Wow," he commented, "that was really something."

The crowd was still, but the hall was filled with an uncanny fetor, as though each of them had loosed an immense, silent fart, which now mingled in a single stench of pure evil. It was one of those moments when hell reaches a kind of pinnacle of awfulness, unparalleled, unsurpassable, the pits.

"Now you must all be asking yourselves," the demonic child continued, "how can *I* help to bring about this new hell on Earth? Well, that's what television is for! Look at this!"

As when, after takeoff, the screens descend throughout the cabin of a 747, a hundred white screens were lowered from their recesses in the ferroconcrete ceiling (the hall, of course, was another creation of hell's resident architect, Philip Johnson). On each screen was a close-up of little Philip Dick, grinning with delight to see himself multiplied so many times.

"What *you* will do is sit there and watch the fatal scene unfold, as though it were the Super Bowl. And I will be your team and you will be my fans and cheer me on, and together we will commit the ultimate act of Treason, and Thomas Disch will die and the Nazis will win World War II, and in the new world that replaces the world that we destroy I will be President! Not George W. Bush: Hell won't need him any more. But me, Philip K. Dick — I will be your president forever!"

The crowd went crazy.

Chapter Thirteen

"I CAN'T GIVE YOU ANYTHING BUT LOVE," is another of those songs addressed to that universal beloved, Baby. Last night watching a library DVD of Puccini's *Il Trittico* I noticed that each of its one-act components is similarly focused on love for a baby or parent, or the lack thereof, as the linchpin of a happy life. Giorgetta only happens into adultery after being traumatized by her infant son's death; Sister Angelica loses the son she'd never known and subsequently her own life; and Lauretta's show-stopper in *Gianni Schicchi*, "O mio babbino caro," has the same timeless message as the song above (and *babbino* — daddy — is only a letter away from *bambino* — baby).

Surely, it's no coincidence that Puccini came from the land of bambini and madonnas, a land where even the nuns sing Liebestods to their little ones. But Italy and Catholicism are scarcely alone in placing parenthood at the top of their To Do lists. Judaism is founded on God's covenant with Abraham that guaranteed his progeny would spread like kudzu. As for Islam, half of all the Muslims in the world right now are teenagers or younger, so fertility would seem to be a top priority there too. Indeed, in proportion as people are without other resources, they breed. That's how immigrant Catholics so quickly became a political force in nineteenth-century America, and how Muslims are taking over the Netherlands now. It is a strategy guaranteed to win so long as nothing is done to stop it.

It's not my concern here to save the Netherlands, or all Europe, from the hordes of the Orient, but rather to suggest my own alternative, one not unlike that of Simeon the Stylite and the other desert fathers (not to mention Mary of Egypt in that Crespi altarpiece): Be gay, don't beget kids, and give Antarctica a chance to breathe. Of course, the desert fathers of the fourth and fifth centuries probably weren't consciously gay, most of them, any more than the Shakers of the nineteenth century. They just had a sense, like William Wordsworth, that the world is too much with us, late and soon, feeding and bleeding. Or in the words of "Father Time," the child suicide/fratricide in Hardy's *Jude the Obscure*: "We were too many."

One needn't be gay to be childless. Indeed, there are gays of both sexes so perverse as to claim the right to sing lullabies to bambini of their own manufacture. The Holy Father has declared himself against that idea, and so do I (with special dispensations, needless to say, for those gay friends of mine who've had children already). My divine injunction is that rather than having children you should concentrate on having fun.

Some pragmatists may counter that this is a short-sighted goal, that breeding many offspring is a form of social security for parents, since you will have a whole throng of heirs to toady to you in your old age. In practice this has not worked out among my own friends who've produced offspring. One such offspring, Dylan Sallis, paid me a visit when he was thirty, wanting to know anything I could tell him about his father, who'd decamped when Dylan was five and would no longer allow the young man visitation rights. I tried to summon some pleasant memories of the Jim

I'd known, but they didn't suffice the boy's needs, and he committed suicide a year later. Not an argument in favor of parenthood.

Other examples are even more dire, but mum's the word, since those offspring are still alive and malfunctioning in spectacular ways. My own *nipoti* (two nieces, two nephews) have been a credit to the family name, but even in their cases one can observe a decline in the philo-progenitive imperative. My father had five kids; those five have had four more; those four have yielded three. This in a family of increasing prosperity. We Disches are, in that sense, Europe writ small, for in none of its nations, from Finland to Italy, are its peoples refilling the niches in the ranks depleted by Death.

Economists often profess to deplore this trend, as prefiguring a decline of the West if not an out-and-out *Götterdämmerung*. From my perspective it will be more like an unusually severe winter.[45] Mankind is not necessarily going to hang on to this planet forever, and surely it would be nobler to exit gracefully than to leave a heap of corpses on the stage, which is the near-future scenario in the background of the opening section in "How the Gods Died." Almost every grown-up I know whose perspective has not been biased by parenthood and its myth of progress anticipates some more or less horrible traffic jam and mad scramble as our civilization nears its finish line, a kind of socioeconomic tsunami that won't stop at the shoreline.

Having hinted at such possibilities in my early parables I was often dismissed as that most un-American of lifeforms, a pessimist or, even worse, a nihilist! I will allow as how I may be reckoned a pessimist (though on the whole a cheerful and *pococurante*

---

45 Not coincidentally, my first novel, *The Genocides* (Berkley, 1965), originally was to have been called *The Long Season*, which in turned morphed into *The Harvest is Past, The Summer is Ended*, a tip of the hat to Jeremiah though it omits his punchline: "…and we are not saved."

sort of pessimist with a healthy not to say voracious appetite), but I am surely no nihilist. I'll go further: I doubt that nihilists exist. They are like vampires and werewolves, a useful libel we can attach to our enemies when we wish to blackball them with no more discussion. I doubt there was any more to it when I was first identified as a nihilist (by Algis Budrys in a 1966 issue of *Galaxy* magazine) than the inflections of my prose style, which a sensitive ear might have registered as gay. Gays were definitely denied entrance to the clubhouse in those days: we were nihilists.

One of my father's favorite jokes, told in a Norwegian accent, was about a fellow who once couldn't spell "engineer" and admits that "now I am one." I'm in the same situation with respect to nihilism. I know: only a paragraph ago I was denying nihilists exist and now I'm signing a confession. Very well, I contradict myself. It's simple, really: I doubt that anyone can truly believe in nothing (though Verdi's Iago makes that claim) because at an epistemological minimum he believes in the Cartesian *cogito*.

The nothing this nihilist believes in (and the one Iago probably had in mind) is the nothing left after all false hopes and delusive dreams have been flensed from our bones, when the constellations overhead have lost all their connective lines and only the random dots are left, when (as in the last chapter) God is dead.

Ivan Karamazov is famed for his very doubtful proposition that if God is dead then anything goes. His dull-witted youngest brother took Ivan at his word and murdered their parent. It's amazing how many people still make that mistake and think that a flirtation with atheism is a gun permit. They are dead wrong. For one thing, atheism is a terrible mistake. Any god would be a fool to say otherwise. God isn't dead; he's with you even as you read these words! Secondly, there are all kinds of non-theological reasons why we should not kill our parents, or ourselves, or our offspring, quite independently of divine prohibitions. There's the penal code. There's elementary psychology and the likelihood of boomeranging guilt (as in *Crime and Punishment*). Suicides, of course, don't suffer remorse, but no one is in more danger of finding they've cut off their nose to spite their face. As to murder of offspring I will admit that the Scriptures[46] often seem to sanction that in particular cases (Abraham and Isaac, Jephtha and his daughter), but even in those cases God and his designated hit men come off looking bad and not a little crazy.

Is crazy another chapter to itself or should we talk about it here? If we think of crazy as an alternative to nihilism, then here's as good a chapter as any. For many zealots — not just Abraham and Jephtha but ordinary off-the-wall weirdos like Phil Dick — crazy is square one. Crazy was that first tab of acid in 1965 and a lifetime of rehabs thereafter. Crazy is never having to say you're sorry, because you're not, and you don't remember what you're supposed to be sorry about, and you can't recognize the person you won't apologize to. Dad, is that you?

Crazy relates to God chiefly in the way that he is a favorite alibi for the crimes committed by crazy people. If you weren't acting under orders from the Devil, then it was God who grabbed hold of your steering wheel. Those who bomb abortion clinics, the defenders of animals' rights, and ayatollahs with a *fatwah* against Salman Rushdie can't be held personally accountable for their crimes because they're acting under orders to see that God's will is done.

I mention these familiar instances of God-ordained felonies only to assure my own worshipers that they will not be called on

---

46 Somewhere on my bookshelves there is an entire volume devoted to divinely-mandated fili-cide in the Hindu religion, but it's not where it should be, next to Hans Torwesten's *Vedanta*. You will just have to believe me.

to be lunatics or assassins on my account. The worst they may have to face is a little ostracism from the terminally humorless, the same people who want Jon Stewart's *America* taken off library shelves or who would keep nine-year-olds from going to Halloween parties costumed as witches and ghosts.

If such a person, finding this book in its hidey-hole down in your den, should get fussed and ask you outright whether you knew that I was Satan or the Antichrist or some other false god, all you need say is, "For heaven's sake, you don't believe *anyone* supposes Tom Disch is God, do you? He's a satirist, and in the worst possible taste!"

Indeed, that may be your own sense of the matter at this juncture, for what actual proof have I produced as to my divinity? I haven't even put together enough blurbs and testimonials from my own true believers to fill the back of a book jacket, though I will in due course make an effort. There are certainly plenty of people who owe me a blurb.

But better than celebrity endorsements are miracles. Nothing so well establishes one's *bona fides* as a god. Christ performed dozens of miracles, helping the lame to walk and the blind to see and putting on a spur-of-the-moment buffet for a horde of picnickers who'd come to one of his happenings. Televangelists have continued that tradition, especially in the medical department. Could I do less?

Chapter Fourteen

APROPOS OF MIRACLES, my own, at first, were inadvertent. It wasn't that I was shy or diffident, like Jesus, who needed a shove from his mother before he miraculously catered the wedding at Cana. It simply hadn't occurred to me till quite late in my career that I had miraculous powers. Even now that I know what I am capable of, I try not to overdo my blessings.

For all that, I do help those who help themselves — usually without their ever knowing they've had a favor from a secret Someone. I shake someone's hand and the plaque that had been piling up in her vena cava dissolves. I blow a kiss and a sinus headache disappears. Sometimes the mere passage of my shadow across his cardboard sign puts steel into the soul of a drug-addicted teenage beggar and he decides to get his GED.

I try to distribute these bounties without too much tipping the scales of divine justice in favor of old friends. Equal opportunity and all that. But the most just god plays favorites from time to time, and a careful audit of the vital statistics of my friends and acquaintances will show some interesting anomalies and deviations from the norm. It's not always simple nepotism on my part. No one wants to spend much time with those whose faces are disfigured with herpes or those cast down by some leaden depression. Miracles that remove warts of that sort I perform as much for my own sake as for my sponsees, as I might brush away cigarette ashes from someone's coat lapel.

Twice I've cured cancer. Once long ago an unsuspected tumor in the kidney of my friend and then editor, Michael Moorcock, who by strange chance had just completed a novel called *A Cure for Cancer*.[47] The second time, more recently, I nuked a much advanced malignancy almost encapsulating the prostate of an editor of the *Sun*, a fledgling New York newspaper for which I was writing occasional reviews of art galleries. In that case the cure was effected by a small wooden nameplate-cum-painting I'd given him as a Christmas present, and the miracle was an unintended consequence of that gift.

I am rather vain about my painting while at the same time aware that it can seem to fall short of the perfection one might expect of a god. I suspect that Jesus may not have been an entirely masterful carpenter. Otherwise would not the basilicas of the world be filled with wonder-working stools and cabinets and armoires, the fruit of his inspired apprenticeship in Joseph's Nazareth carpenter shop?

What a lovely notion for a novel in the vein of Lloyd Douglas's *The Robe*! *The Cedar Chest: A Tale of the Teenage Christ*. Any clothes kept in the chest would endow the wearers with a measure of supernatural grace in proportion to the time they'd lain inside. Thus, there could be a succession of happy Scrooge-like transformations: prodigal sons and reformed thieves, repentant harlots and born-again slave-owners, all wearing seamless garments that

---

47 *A Cure for Cancer* (Alison and Busby, 1971). An earlier Moorcock novel from 1969, *Behold the Man*, offers a kind of mirror image to *The Word of God* in that it tells of a Moorcock-like time traveler who searches for the historical Christ in old Jerusalem and ends up taking his place on Calvary. The book was dedicated to me!

carry a lingering scent of heaven from that chest formed by His hands.

I digress, but not that widely, for it was a painting of mine that acted as the conduit for my most effective and long-lasting miracle, as, hanging in her sickroom (or stored in her attic) for some two decades, it sustained the life of my friend Virginia Kidd.

All those who knew Virginia in her later years must be aware that there was something miraculous in her longevity. Born in 1921 and a charter member of the Futurian clan of SF writers in the 1940s, Virginia was already, when I first met her in 1964, an immensely fat woman for whom any staircase presented a challenge she was seldom inclined to meet. She was then living in a tumbledown old house in Milford, Pennsylvania, that the federal government had taken possession of with a thought to its submersion when it had dammed the Delaware and erased the lower-lying parts of Milford from the map. The dam never happened and Virginia lingered on paying a nominal rent for the use of the house she'd been dispossessed of. In such circumstances one stints on capital improvements, so the house became ever more derelict even as Virginia became ever more sedentary. When her children were teenagers they enjoyed an uncommon degree of independence, for their mother never ventured into the upper regions of the house — or anywhere that required a departure of more than two steps from the horizontal plane on which she permanently resided. She could drive her car to the post office and the grocery, and she knew which local restaurants were stairless and otherwise equipped to accommodate her needs.

Within those limits Virginia enjoyed a comfortable and even affluent life, as the literary agency she founded in the late 1960s grew and prospered. The creaky old house emptied of children and filled with the agency's employees and Virginia's personal caregivers. She ventured out of the house less and less often, and (having grown heavier) was seldom out of the large mechanical bed that also served as an office chair. Virginia was among the first to welcome the computer age, and the Internet had not been in existence for a nanosecond before Virginia became a round-the-clock resident of the global village. She was the first person I knew with a dedicated phone line so she could always plug in to her alternate CompuServe universe.

Some women don't reveal their age; Virginia didn't say what she weighed, though we all wondered. What does the soprano Jane Eaglen weigh? Virginia must have weighed fifty pounds more. Her doctors were always putting her on diets, but in that, as in the matter of cigarettes, Virginia went her own way. She told tales against herself, marveling merrily at the time she'd awaken to discover that somehow she'd cooked and eaten a whole pot of spaghetti during one nighttime raid on the pantry. She gloried in her appetite as an athlete in his prowess, and all who dined with her pigged out with a special zest, emboldened by the tacit permission of her own dauntless appetite.

How it was that Virginia came to see the painting that would sustain her so long I can't now recall. I had yet to move to Barryville and become her near neighbor, and in any case she never visited me in Barryville, where she might have seen it, for by that time she was anchored to her bed. Perhaps she'd praised the painting years earlier, on a visit to New York. It was painted in 1975, as I began to write *On Wings of Song*, for which it had been conceived as a kind of illustration. In the upper left corner is a diver suspended (in fact, flying) over a pastoral patchwork of green woodlands and amber fields of grain: "The Diver" can be understood as a portrait of the book's hero (and flattering mirror image) Daniel Weinreb. It's a nice design, although the execution is unskilled and lazy (which is the charge that my partner and most candid critic Charles Naylor levels against *all* my paintings), but Virginia, bless her, enthused over it as though she could see it through my own rose-colored glasses. Such praise may be expected from one's own mother, even one's agent, but Virginia was only an old friend. I gave her the painting from sheer puppy-dog gratitude, and it hung there in her bedroom/office for years, an emblem of my own vaulting and misguided ambition and that of my whole tribe of highbrow science fiction writers, the so-called Milford Mafia.

Years it hung there as we all grew old — myself, Virginia, and her list of clients that included Ursula Le Guin, R. A. Lafferty, Joanna Russ, and Michael Swanwick. I summered in the neighborhood from 1983 on and finally settled in Barryville in 1992, at which time Virginia agreed to let me bring over my easel and attempt her portrait. A portrait of Virginia would be a challenge even to Sir Joshua Reynolds. Fat people are as vain as all the rest of us, and Virginia spent a pretty penny having a woman come in to do her nails and hair. She trusted my paintbrush to accomplish a similar feat of beautification. I had studied at the Art Students League since painting "The Diver" and figured I'd be up to the job.

I still think it's not half bad: larger even than in life, the hectic pink of her face has the glow of a Murillo madonna; her eyes are lifted heavenward with a similar artless rapture; all this above the turquoise sea of her great bosom. The thin brown hair is rendered with a few exigent brushstrokes deft as any beautician's. Behind her an ivy unlooses a little cartouche of leaves against a ground of day-glow yellow. She was the angel of a transcendental obesity.

But Virginia did not entertain the same high estimate of my painting and declined to accept it as a gift. However, she did keep "The Diver" hanging in her bedroom — and "The Diver" kept her alive. It was no easy task. Virginia was in and out of the hospital all through her sixties and seventies. The doctors put her on various regimens; she drank her dinners from cans; she griped and whined and begged her bedside visitors to smuggle in forbidden pleasures, be it only a few potato chips. Through it all she never seemed to lose an ounce. From being a blessing, "The Diver" had become a curse. Neither the years of smoking and overeating nor the shock of her new cruel deprivations would let her shuffle off her mortal coil, though that was the consummation she now devoutly wished. "The Diver" hung there, and so did Virginia by a slender unbreakable thread.

Finally she was released by sheer accident. One of the agency employees, unaware of the painting's life-sustaining power but taking a fancy to it *qua* painting, transferred "The Diver" to her own office upstairs, where it exerted a much diminished influence. At last, with a sigh of thanks, Virginia, at the age of eighty-one, passed away on January 10, 2003.

I reclaimed "The Diver" from the agency (supposing it fated to moulder in the agency's attic) and hung it in my own pantry, an annex to the kitchen into which my clothes dryer vents its linty hot air. The picture no longer tickled my vainglory as it had at age forty-two, but there was something about it that kept me from relegating it to the darker, unvisited oblivion of the attic. Every few weeks I would wipe away the latest film of lint and find myself trammeled by a charm more elemental than that of any art. The painting, like one of Chartres's great stained glass windows, became my gateway to another realm — to an appreciation of my own awesome divinity and supernatural powers.

I am not alone among science fiction writers in possessing powers of healing, teleportation, and prophecy. Walt and Leigh Richmond, who also lived in Milford at one time, had diverse and well-developed psychic powers. On my very first visit to Milford in

1964 I stayed with the Richmonds and watched Walt diagnose and cure the trick knee of a writer my own age. The Richmonds, having telepathic powers, had found a uniquely effective way to collaborate as writers: Walt would *project* his vision of their tales to Leigh, who served the humble albeit indispensable role of his amanuensis. Philip Dick, in his later years, was in direct contact with something divine or extraterrestrial that used him as its pipeline to other inhabitants of the mortal realm.[48] Whitley Strieber, in addition to his widely heralded ordeals as an alien abductee, has mastered the art of out-of-body flight.[49] As to prophetic powers, you name it, we've predicted it! Prophetic power is our forte.

So in revealing myself to be a god, I am not claiming that much more than many others in the sf community. Admittedly, it may strike many at first as a bold claim, even immodest, but really it is a mainstream American ambition with many antecedents. Ann Lee, Ralph Waldo Emerson, Mary Baker Eddy, Joseph Smith, L. Ron Hubbard, Charlie Manson — they've all been there before me, links in one golden chain, steps in one vast celestial staircase, and all of them ready to invite their fellow countrymen to join them in the big tent of their mystic invention.

As I invite you, my readers. Have you a need you'd like to whisper in my ear? Are you lonely, depressed, anxious, unpopular, unable to concentrate? I can help you. Are you stuck in a nowhere job? Married the wrong spouse? Do you think suicide may be the only solution to your problems? Ah, you mustn't think that! There is another way. Just follow the path you are already on. Read to the end of this book and the great burden you bear will be lifted.

48   For a full account of Dick's close encounters with the Other, the Unnameable, and the Unimaginable (he goes by many names) read *VALIS* (Bantam, 1981, and soon to be a major motion picture), as well his more ambitious theological tract, the "Exegesis," selections from which have been published in *In Pursuit of VALIS*. (Underwood-Miller, 1991).
49   *Transformation: The Breakthrough* (Morrow, 1988).

I can't tell you how at this point. If I did, the process would be nullified, the way a birthday wish is forfeited if you don't keep it sealed inside your heart.

You've come so far already. We're almost at the end of Chapter Fourteen. Everyone becomes a little impatient at that point, but the end is in sight, and I can promise not only that it will be a happy ending, but that in reaching it you will obtain good health, new vigor, and a peace of mind as calm and bright as cumulus on an April morning.

Come to me! Surrender the burden of your self! Adore!

Chapter Fifteen

On the Road

"SO WHERE ARE WE GOING?" Fletch asked the kid beside him in the passenger seat of the next-to-new Chevy the kid had just paid for (Fletch had fronted as the official purchaser) with a tidy two grand in crisp hundred-dollar bills fresh from the track. (And that was just a fraction of the kid's winnings!)

"To Minneapolis," the kid answered.

"And that's...where exactly?" Fletch, with the help of his fifty-cent Cuban cigar (also fresh from the track), managed to give the question a smart-guy tone.

The kid tilted his head and rolled up his eyes, like everyone in the world was supposed to have a road map of the whole country inside his head. Fletch hated the little fucker's guts, and he was in half a mind to spread them out on the back seat of the car once they hit the highway, but only after a thorough rectal exam. Fletch had developed a taste for chicken while he was doing time in San Quentin.

"Minneapolis is in Minnesota, Fletcher. Right on the 45th parallel."

"And around the corner from the North Pole, yeah right. I knew that, I just forgot."

"It's a little over two thousand miles from here. I figure it'll take us about thirty-six hours if I spell you with the driving."

Fletch whistled, a mode of expression he had yet to master perfectly at the age of forty-one, though not for want of earnest application. "With *you* driving? Is that some kind of joke?"

"I'll drive at night. It won't be a problem."

The kid was such a nervy little bastard, but he might well be as good a driver as Fletch, who never had been able to pass the license exams in Texas, Utah, or California. He'd always messed up on the written part before he even had a chance to get behind the wheel and show his stuff. It wasn't his fault really. They don't have Driver's Ed classes in Quentin, plus he'd had a lot of bad luck. Maybe in Minneapolis his luck would get better. God knows the kid was a regular four-leaf clover of good luck.

Still, Fletch felt obliged to protest. Taking orders from a damned twelve-year-old (which was what the kid claimed to be) was worse than taking orders from a woman. "Your parents are going to be calling the police, kid. You'll be a missing person. And if I drive you across the state line I could be in deep shit. Forgive the language."

It was not like Fletch to make apologies, but this kid could be his meal ticket if he played his cards right. He didn't want to queer his chances this early in the game. And the idea of getting two thousand miles away from Oakland had something to recommend it independent of everything else. Fletch was a wanted man.

"It's forgiven, Fletcher, and forgotten already. Now let's get a move on. We had a big lunch at the drive-in, so we should be able to get to Reno before we have to stop to eat again. Time is of the essence."

Time is of the essence! Jesus, where did the kid come up with that stuff! He talked like some college professor. Then it dawned on him: they'd be going through Reno.

"Reno's on the way, is it? Maybe we'll have time to hit the slots?"

"Sure thing, Fletcher — a minute or two. Why? Are you feeling lucky?" The kid smiled in his know-it-all way and touched the frames of his thick glasses, adjusting them.

Fletch knew the kid was being sarcastic. The luck was all on the kid's side, and Fletch was just along for the ride. But sometimes being along for the ride is all the luck a person needs.

"Okay," said Fletch, caving. "We go to Minneapolis. But when we get there I get this car, right?"

"That's the deal. The papers are already in your name, you know that."

"You also said that when we get there I got to do you a couple favors."

"For which you will be amply rewarded. Now no more questions, please. I'd like to listen to the radio."

"Okay, just one thing. I don't know your name."

"It's Philip. Call me Phil, if you like."

"Philip what?"

The kid touched his glasses again, as though they were a Halloween mask that kept slipping down his nose. "Philip K. Roth."

Roth — it sounded like a Jewish name to Fletch. *Now* things were starting to make sense. Kikes were always lucky with money. That's how the kid had picked one winner after another at the track. "So — you're Jewish?" Fletch asked, trying to make it sound like a compliment.

The kid shook his head. "It's just an American name, like yours, Mr. Nesbit."

Fletch fiddled with his cigar, which had developed a sour taste, and tried to remember when he'd told the kid his real name instead of the name on his fake driver's license, Fletcher Scott. Was the kid some kind of mind reader? "You call me Fletcher, I'll call you Phil, and we'll be pals. Okay?"

"Heigh-ho," said Philip Roth.

"Okay, let's hit the road."

All his years in hell had given Phil a new appreciation of the classic American landscape of highway, wasteland, and urban blight, the vistas celebrated with such headlong rapture by Jack Kerouac in the once and future fifties. When he'd first read *On the Road* Phil had felt only contempt, envy, and leaden dismay. What could the reading public be thinking to make that over-blown travelogue a best-seller, that teenager hotrodder's hymn to the poisonous fruits of a soulless, capitalist consumer society! And just at the time when his own first works of fiction were appearing in print, books that celebrated the Space Age just then aborning. *On the Road* had premiered in 1957, the same year *Eye in the Sky*, his own first adventure in cosmogenic solipsism, saw print, a work that dwarfed Kerouac's conceptually and every other way except for the RPMs of the prose. Later, in the seventies, living in a hippie commune, smashed on speed, Phil had listened to a stoned Deadhead read aloud from Kerouac's sacred text and had finally realized what all the fuss was about. Kerouac's prose was like the first rush of meth when the world around you begins accelerating and flashing by in streaks of orange neon, like the Vegas strip the first time you cruise through on acid, like a whole whorehouse of preteen Lolitas in the glory days of Haight-Ashbury. And Lord, did Phil hate John Ashbery, even more than Kerouac. Phil hadn't even *heard* of Ashbery till he got to hell and married Joycelin who *adored* Ashbery and would read him aloud in the nasal monotone she reserved for only the deadliest bores.

He was free! He wasn't in hell any more, he was in the America of 1939, when Joycelin hadn't even been born. Or Thomas M. Fucking Disch either. And if Phil could help it, he never would be! The Disch gamete and Mann gamete, like East and West, would never meet. And Phil would rule in the kingdom of Dick. He began to sing:

> *In Dick's sweet land*
> *I'll take my stand*
> *To live and die in Dixie.*
> *Away! away!*
> *Away down south in Dixie*

"Hey kid," said Fletcher at the wheel of the Chevy, "if you're awake, would you reach into that bag on the floor and take out a pack of Camels. This cigar is *dead.*"

"Good idea," said Phil. He fumbled around inside the bag among the candy bars and inhalers and dug out a pack of cigarettes. They'd stocked up on all kinds of travel necessities at the truck stop outside of Pocatello, including the very latest issue of *Astounding* with a Schneeman cover showing a pair of astronauts against a backdrop of Saturn's rings. The paper was as white and fresh and supple as the dollar bills he'd won at the track. April 1939! It was the *point d'appui* that Archimedes talked about, where you could lift the whole world with the right lever in place, the *Zusammenklapbarzeit*, the hinge-moment when empires are won or lost with the roll of the dice. And he'd be that lever, he'd throw those dice.

Phil unzipped the cellophane, wiggled two cigarettes free, and lit them. One he handed to Fletcher, the other was his. The first drag was like another mouthful of the banana cream pie he'd ordered at the Pocatello diner. There was nothing like the joys of the flesh.

"You look like you're a regular smoker," said Fletcher with a sideways glance.

"So do you," said Phil. "And we should both be ashamed of ourselves. Cigarettes cause cancer, you know."

"Bullshit," said Fletcher. "Who told you that?"

Phil just smiled. He loved 1939. It was as though it wasn't just him who was a child — it was a whole country full of dumb bunnies. The programs on the radio! The wheezy jokes and brain-damaged songs! Even the haircuts. Fletcher's was priceless, like Moe in the *Three Stooges* comedies. Imagine paying someone to make you look like that.

Outside the car was a darkness absolute as hell's, except for the flicker of the median strip as it zipped forward into the Chevy's lights. Clouds cloaked the stars, and there hadn't been a car in the westbound lane for at least five minutes. They might have been the last men left on Earth. Always such a lovely idea. Racing to Minneapolis to rape the last woman.

For just a moment Phil experienced that old jolt of *Eureka!* he used to get when a new idea came to him. But almost immediately the jolt faded to a tickle at the back of his throat and then a cough. The Phil from hell might be used to three packs a day but the ten-year-old from Zebulon Pike Elementary had tenderer flesh.

"Smoke six packs," Fletcher said, echoing the ad they'd heard on the radio a couple of hours earlier, "and find out why Camels are the largest-selling cigarette in America."

"Oh, shut up and drive," said Phil, whose eyes had started tearing from the smoke.

"Sure thing, kid. Whatever you say."

At the next truck stop, a diner outside Hot Springs, South Dakota, Phil watched Fletcher do something he hadn't seen since he was fifteen back at Pacific High. He took the top off one of the Breathe-Way inhalers and tickled out one of the strips of paper accordioned into the bottle. Then he dunked the paper inside his cup of milky coffee, stirred in three spoons of sugar, and swallowed down the concoction in long, slow sips. Before he'd entirely polished it off, he offered the dregs of the cup to Phil.

Phil never said no to a new pharmaceutical adventure. He didn't even ask what they were taking. It had to be Benzedrine, which had been available over-the-counter well into the Fifties. Guys at Pacific High would stock up on inhalers a dozen at a time. For any serious distance on the road a supply of Benzedrine was as necessary as the fuel in the tank.

Phil had taken the wheel through the latter, flatter half of Wyoming, while Fletcher had dozed. Now it was Fletcher's turn again, and Phil, to maintain the momentum of their journey, soliloquized. He never was so careless as to let slip that he was on an embassy from hell, but he couldn't resist fucking with Fletcher's addled mind in smaller ways. Fletcher had been unwise enough to make some snide remarks about Phil's talismanic issue of *Astounding* ("Where's that, the Moon? And who's that in the spacesuit — Princess Alura?"), which gave Phil all he needed to launch into a whole spiel on how outer space was the next frontier and how there would be a race to see which country would be the first to land a man on the Moon.

"Like a horse race, huh? And who's going to be at the starting

gate? Let me guess. Germany. America. Japan. And…France?"

Phil realized Fletcher had just stumbled into Phil's own copyrighted territory: an alternate America in the wake of an Axis victory when Germany and Japan, not America and Russia, had pioneered the conquest of space, an America divided into German and Japanese zones of occupation, the way Germany had been split in two after its defeat. The United States now stood on the brink of the most cataclysmic war of all time, but most people were still trying to pretend that the inevitable could be sidestepped, that Germany would content itself with a few scraps of Poland, that America could stay on the sidelines whatever happened in Europe. In the whole country only ten-year-old Philip K. Dick knew what would really happen, how in just a week or two German tanks would roll across the borders of Poland and push on to Warsaw as fast as America's legions smashed through Iraq. Then, like dominos, Norway and Denmark, Belgium and Holland and finally France would all collapse before the assault of the German juggernaut. Finally only the United States would stand in the way of Hitler's total conquest of Europe. He would be the Napoleon of the twentieth century, the Augustus Caesar of a thousand-year German Imperium.

And Phil had seen it all, that alternative future of a triumphant Third Reich. All the way back in 1961, when Kennedy was partying with Marilyn Monroe in the White House, Phil's amphetamine-enflamed mind had seen the terrible Might-Have-Been that now, in 1939, was still a possibility. It all lay in his hands, whether the Moving Finger of Fate could be persuaded to rewrite a few lines of history, and then a few more, and finally revise the entire text! Who could resist attempting a task so heroic, the biggest crapshoot of all time? Whatever might happen to himself in such a topsy-turvy world (and he *had* been promised the presidency!), he would have wrought changes and wreaked havoc on a scale to vie with Alexander or the conquistadores. Who could say no to that?

And so, as they zoomed like some four-wheel rocket across the Badlands of South Dakota, Phil played the role of Scheherazade, spinning out tales (which he ascribed to the authors of *Astounding*) of Man's conquest of the stars, of robots and giant worms, and then (the speedometer was up to 70 MPH and Fletcher's eyes were glazed) of Germany's certain victory over France with its ruling cabal of Rothschild bankers and Communist goons.

The mark of Cain fairly blazed on the boy's brow.

Chapter Sixteen

PHIL DICK was not the only artist of the sixties who offered his sanity on the altar of art in the hope that it would be a sacrifice savory to the nostrils of the gods. We were all ready to fry our brains back then if it would make us geniuses, or even if it would make us feel rapturously brainy for a little while. That was the premise of my own novel from 1968, *Camp Concentration*, which so impressed Phil that he wrote me a fan letter inquiring, in effect, where *he* could get hold of some of my imaginary wonder drug, and which inspired him a little later to denounce me to the FBI. I still have his letter in my files, and the FBI has his other letter in theirs, where Phil's biographer unearthed it using the Freedom of Information Act.

The love of psychoactive drugs was not just a fashion of the sixties. The Lost Generation of the Jazz Age — Hemingway, Fitzgerald, Steinbeck, Faulkner — all wrote their hymns to Bacchus and wound up hungover, working for Hollywood, and the worse for wear. Gen-Xers of the nineties fueled their delusions with cocaine and whatever else was at hand. A little later it was ecstasy, and now all through Middle America and the Bible Belt drug fashions have come full circle, and we're back to home-brewed Benzedrine, or "crystal" as it's called now.

Indeed, the need is timeless. As Dylan sang, "Everybody must get stoned." Not just the Lost and the Beat Generations, not just today's trailer trash, not just Phil in his Benzedrine rocketship, but Pentheus in Euripides's "The Bacchae,"[50] François Villon, Thomas de Quincey (famed for the *Confessions of an English Opium-Eater*), and that most popular and accessible of German poets, Heinrich Heine, who wrote the following poem in praise of the drug he was addicted to:

Morphine

Two brothers there are: Sleep and Death,
Both handsome as hell, though one's more pale,
With an air of military discipline.
The other, who holds me in his loose embrace,
Is common by comparison, rough trade
Almost. But such a smile, and such a gaze.
While we lie here I'll confess
The halo of hair about his brow
Is purest uncut heroin, exquisite
To touch, so silken and so petal soft — but also,
Alas, so evanescent. It is only when the whiter twin,
Who never seems to smile, snuffs
His candle and sets it down
That one may know true peace.

---

50 Adapted as "Dionysus in '69" this play toured the country for a couple years like a countercul-ture revival. At each performance the audience was invited to join the bacchanal of naked, freaked-out thespians on the stage. I was one of those who answered Dionysus's summons, strutted my brief hour on the stage, and had a marvelously gaga and tragically brief love affair as a result. I can still heave a sigh at the memory.

Sleep is good but better Death.
The best is never to have breathed at all.[51]

In Heine's time no one had yet thought to make drugs more enticing by drawing up laws against them, and so all sorts of respectable middle-class types like Heine were hard-core stoners: Coleridge, Mrs. Carlyle, Poe, Thoreau, Cocteau, and so on up to Yoko Ono in our own time.

Like those forms of sex not consecrated by the rite of matrimony, drug use has generally been a guilty pleasure, though not *so* guilty that it hasn't accumulated its own literature and roster of celebrity endorsements. Wine, of course, has had legions of praise-singers. The Beats, but especially Burroughs, have been there for most mind-altering drugs. But the great sensation of the sixties was LSD, and that drug's poet laureate was Aldous Huxley, author of *The Doors of Perception* and *Heaven and Hell*. Huxley acted as a one-man public relations agency for lysergic acid diethylamide, averring in a tone of sober eloquence, that LSD acted to dissolve the usual partitions between common sense and celestial vision, making all men shamans and seers. One's acid trips weren't just ravishingly beautiful but on some metaphysical level *true*. Those shimmering Xanadus and diamond-studded skies were authentically divine — and therefore LSD (its devotees argued) should enjoy the same First Amendment privileges as the paraphernalia of other religions. After all, peyote, LSD's first cousin, was already recognized as a sacrament of the Native American religion. All we were saying was give acid a chance.

Many thousands of brains had to be fried to a crisp before the audience took a step backward and had a second thought. Some of

---

51 "Morphine" by Heinrich Heine, translated by Felix H. Disch, hitherto unpublished.

acid's chief advocates, such as Timothy Leary, went to jail; others self-destructed on their own. One of the most vivid cautionary tales of the post-psychedelic era was Phil Dick's. His own drug of choice wasn't acid, but few have ever chronicled the phantasms and quicksands of a bad trip more rippingly than Dick. To cite only a few of the dozens of tales and novels that formed Dick's one-man Library of Adventures in Pharmacopeia: *Martian Time-Slip*, "Faith of Our Fathers," *Ubik*, *Flow My Tears, The Policeman Said*, VALIS, and *The Three Stigmata of Palmer Eldritch*.

Even if he were not already in the cast of the drama now playing in this theater, Phil would merit an honorable mention in this chapter for the way in which he epitomized a sea change in the religion of his country. Phil, in his work and in his life, confronted a god radically unlike the Supreme Being that had been worshipped by organized religions in the organ-playing churches of the pre-Dick era, the god whose names and attributes were laid down in doctrinal specifications that councils and synods had given their seal of approval to. Dick, like today's evangelicals, had a *personal*, one-on-one relationship with his god. He and his god spoke the same language, saw the same movies, and shared joints. Phil's god might also speak from a whirlwind at times, or from a burning bush; he could be devious and cruel, a rather Manichaean god (or a matched set); a gnostic god, too, when gnostic gods came to be the fashion. But what Phil insisted on (like President Bush and today's more flexible Pentecostals) was a god he could relate to in an I'm Okay/You're Okay way.

Among his other agreeable attributes, such a god is an ideal deity for a ventriloquist, a man with the confidence to speak on behalf of the god he worships. If mediums at a séance can speak in the voices of those who have passed to the other side, is it any greater wonder that gods should have their spokespersons? In his learned treatise on this subject, *The Prophetic Faith*,[52] Martin Buber declares that the defining characteristic of the true biblical prophet, or *nabi*, is that he speaks "mouth to mouth" with God and is thus a cut above the *nebiim*, who know the deity only through visions. In this conception God's breath and his prophet's are one.

This is, of course, the Romantic view of the poet's mission: poets are God's own Aeolian harps, yielding music as the breath of god's zephyrs sweeps their strings. Like Shelley's skylark they are not subject to gravity, but

> *Higher still and higher*
> *From the earth thou springest,*
> *Like a cloud of fire*
> *The blue deep thou wingest,*
> *And singing still dost soar, and soaring ever singest.*[53]

On the one occasion I met Phil, on a visit to his condo in Anaheim in September of 1974, when he was in high *nabi* gear, full of tales of how God had been rattling his cupboard and sending angelic visitors disguised as fetching nymphets. VALIS was around the corner but in a still unassembled state, like Phil himself. I shared his bong and listened respectfully, as to the Delphic pythoness, but I could not affirm Phil's vision in terms *he* would have initialed. I remarked on the various ways his testimony accorded with the major Romantic poets, both English and German, but while he nodded a wary acceptance of such compliments he persisted in seeking a more complete submission. How could I

---

52   *The Prophetic Faith* by Martin Buber (Macmillan, 1949)
53   "To A Skylark" from *Prometheus Unbound* by Percy Bysshe Shelley (C & J Ollier, 1820)

account for his command of Demotic Greek in his dreams? How had he diagnosed his son's hernia, when it had escaped the notice of doctors? When I parted from my host for a visit to Disneyland, I felt like someone leaving Dracula's castle without having given blood. His hunger to be believed was that palpable.

Phil could not have known at that time (since I did not) that I was the one person least likely to put credence in his theophanies, being a god myself. I was much more curious about the writerly side of his life than his mystic revelations, but while he let slip a few fascinating tidbits (for instance, how his second wife Anne had helped him in interpreting the *I Ching*'s directions for the plot of *The Man in the High Castle*, becoming, in effect, his collaborator), he could not be coaxed to pursue those themes but kept returning to his new apocrypha.

It seems appropriate that someone so determined to be recognized as a prophet should have enjoyed his greatest successes posthumously, both in the high-budget films of recent and forthcoming years, which continue to keep his name alive and enrich his heirs, and also, retroactively, in the Minneapolis of 1939, in the hallways and bedrooms of the Leamington Hotel to which we return in the next chapter.

Chapter Seventeen

Room Service

"OH," HELEN SAID RESPECTFULLY, "that is just so…lovely."

They stood before the parted curtains looking out at the night skyline of Minneapolis. The old gentleman had one hand on the curtain's drawstring, the other on his mustache, as though to conceal his smile. Helen was sure he was smiling at her ooing and ahing as though they were on the observation deck of the Foshay Tower instead of the third floor of the Leamington Hotel, but the city really was a beautiful sight with the windows of so many of the office buildings still lit up and a mist making everything dim and mysterious. She felt like an actress in a movie.

"It is lovely," the old gentleman agreed. "And in much the way you are, my dear Chantal."

She winced, and wished she'd never invented a name that was so obviously made-up. The way the old man pronounced it it sounded like a word in a foreign language, which just underlined how *she* would never qualify as a Chantal. She might just as well have told him her name was Fifi, or Aurelia. (Though she actually had a sister-in-law by that name.)

"You are young, and this city is young, as well. I doubt that any of the edifices we are looking at would have been here fifty years ago."

"Really?" Helen said, not believing him but having no evidence to offer as to the city's greater antiquity. "I suppose where you come from everything is older."

"Well, these things are relative, aren't they? Wiesbaden is surely a few centuries older than Minneapolis, but most of its principal buildings date from the nineteenth century, when it became a popular watering place, like Bath in England."

Helen nodded knowingly, though she'd never heard of Wiesbaden or Bath in England. You almost had to laugh at the idea of a popular "watering place" called Bath.

"In a perspective of history Wiesbaden is not that much older than Minneapolis. Measured against Rome or Athens or the Pyramids of Egypt it is but an older sister of your Foshay Tower."

"Have you been to those places?" Helen asked, hoping to change the subject of Minneapolis.

"To Rome, certainly, as a tourist, but never, sad to say, to Athens. As for Egypt, not so long ago I had tickets to sail from Trieste to Alexandria, but finally, in the present unsettled state of the world, that did not seem a wise undertaking. Perhaps if I had been younger? But I came here instead."

"To Minneapolis? Well, you won't see any pyramids here."

He emitted a polite little cough of a laugh, just like Red's mother when her husband made a remark she knew he meant to be funny. But the old woman didn't have any other, more natural laugh, whereas Mr. Hesse had a nice almost musical-sounding laugh for something that genuinely tickled him. In just their little time together Helen had come to like the old guy a lot. His stiffness and old-fashioned good manners were only skin-deep. What was likeable about him, and very unusual, was that he actually seemed to listen to what someone else said, and think about it. She wondered if that was usually the case with people from Europe.

"I did not mean that I came to Minneapolis, specifically," he replied. "I meant the United States in general. I've been here some months now, and seen many cities, and even the older cities on the Atlantic coast seem quite young, because the newer buildings so much dominate the landscape. In most German cities the center of the city is dominated by its *Dom*, its cathedral. Later builders have politely deferred to the church's preeminence when they built. Here the churches are dwarfed by office towers and even the great hotels. This is the utopia of commerce. I imagine your Foshay Tower is just the premonition of the grandeur of the Minneapolis to come. By the year 2000 the view from this window — if the Leamington has been left standing — will offer a panorama of skyscrapers across the whole horizon, and the Foshay Tower will not be the biggest of them."

"If you say so, but the year 2000 is a long way off."

"True enough. I won't live to see my prophetic gifts put to the test, but you, dear Chantal, might well do so. Eighty is not an uncommon age to attain to in these days of sulfonamides and other wondrous drugs."

Helen did the mental arithmetic quickly and smiled to think that the old gentleman was supposing her to be twenty years old. Of course, by his reckoning there wouldn't be that much difference between twenty and twenty-three. No one would ask to see *his* identification when he went into a bar.

Just then there was a knock on the door. The old man looked annoyed and pulled the curtains closed. "That will be Klaus, and we have no need of *him* here and now, do we, my dear?" He patted Helen's hands, which had clenched about the glass that had held her Manhattan. Now only an orange slice remained, and the stem of the maraschino cherry. All she could think of was being caught in the old gent's room by the hotel management. But she hadn't done anything wrong. Hotel guests were entitled to have visitors. All very true, but in her imagination she had already been hauled into the police station on Hennepin Avenue and was being finger-printed.

Thomas went to the door with every intention of dismissing his son with a peremptory "*Verschwindet!*" but when he opened the door it wasn't Klaus standing there but a child (or a dwarf?) attired in the Leamington's livery and supporting on his shoulder an ice bucket and a bottle of champagne on a silver-plated tray.

"Herr Hesse?" the lad inquired.

"Yes…but I don't believe I ordered anything from room service." Even as he made this demur Thomas realized how well-suited to his present purpose a bottle of champagne would be. What likelier tool to deploy in undermining Chantal's virginal modesty? Champagne had been serving such a purpose time out of mind, and *this* champagne had the further virtue in that it seemed to have been imported from the pages of his own "Felix Krull,"[54] a bottle of *Deutschland's* tawdriest forgery, Lorely Extra Cuvée, complete with an ersatz coat of arms and silver wire securing its cork. Lord knows what the Leamington management must charge for such *vin inférieur.*

"Oh, you didn't order this, sir. It's with the compliments of someone who *phoned* just now and said to send it to your room. Shall I open it, sir?"

"To be sure," Thomas said (thinking, "Ah that sly Klaus!"). "To be sure."

---

54 "Felix Krull" appears in Mann's *Stories of Three Decades* (Knopf, 1936) and later became the basis of his last novel, *Confessions of Felix Krull, Confidence Man.*

Only when the boy had gone inside (and seen Chantal) did it occur to him to ask: "And is there a note to say who my well-wisher is?"

"Only this," the boy said, setting the tray and its burden on the glass-capped rosewood table that stood before the peony-blazoned sofa. He held up a tired red tea rose, from which, at this exertion, a single petal floated to the floor. He turned to la belle Chantal and presented the rose to her with a click of his little heels and a deferential *"Fräulein!"* Such a fine little actor: he might have been an understudy at a grand hotel in Paris. Then, puffing out his chest like a pigeon, he spread apart the silver-wire seal and placed a white napkin over the bottle of champagne. With a lewd wink at Thomas, he slid his upraised thumbs to either side of the concealed cork, and asked, "Shall we?"

Who could resist such an impudent little Cherubino? He was, if anything, a more enticing package than dear Chantal.

"Mais oui!" Thomas consented.

Either he was in the first delirium of infatuation or the boy had actually caught his little bilingual word play. Or did his little smirk have some other reference point? The boy's thumbs began to tease the cork up from the neck of the bottle, and his eyes engaged with Thomas's.

Thomas was getting an erection. Most embarrassing, and most gratifying as well. Not that there was any possibility, here in Minneapolis, of taking so much as a sip from the cup. Even in Venice, his von Aschenbach could only gaze on his beloved Tadzio. But how alike they were, this bellhop and Tadzio, even down to the detail of the dark blue gilt-buttoned jacket with cap to match. And the smile! Thomas remembered his own exemplary prose on the theme of Tadzio's smile, a little hymn to Eros: "It was a smile unblushing yet inviting; a speaking, winning, captivating smile with slowly parting lips. With such a smile it might be that Narcissus bent over the mirror of the pool to whisper his endearments."[55]

The cork exploded from the bottle and fell, together with the napkin, to the carpet.

Chantal, who had made a ritual squeal of excitement, and burbled, "Oh, Mister Hesse, you shouldn't of! A whole bottle of champagne for just the two of us."

The boy — Narcissus/Tadzio/Cherubino — had managed to position the frothing bottle over one crystal flute and then, spilling not a drop, the other. To what institute of training were youths sent where they could learn such essential skills? Somewhere in Paris it must be — and with that thought the author awakened in Thomas and he conceived an entire and inevitable novel, which he would have to write as soon as he had finished the last of the Joseph novels. It would be an extension of the tale of Felix Krull from ever so long ago, his mock-*Bildungsroman* of the education of an artist, except that the artist in this case would be a confidence artist, a trickster, whose entire art lay in the charm by which he lured his victims — the guests in some *Belle Époque* hotel in Paris where he worked, like this sweet child, as a bellboy, bowing and scraping and wheedling gratuities and offering his tight little ass for sale.

The boy handed one of the champagne flutes to Chantal and the other to Thomas. "*Prost!*" he declared, which Thomas repeated and then Chantal.

They were doomed.

They were doomed, Phil thought with a shiver of the most delicious guilt. The years he'd spent along the Styx had changed him from the lukewarm liberal with the occasional streak of unmo-

55 *Stories of Three Decades* by Thomas Mann (Knopf, 1936)

tivated meanness, to a full-fledged Iago. "Evil, be thou my good," was his working motto, but evil on any scale can be a hard goal to achieve in hell, where evil has already been maximized and one's own sufferings take up most of one's attention. Back here on Earth Phil's range of hurtful action was so much wider, and his malice could be directed against the guileless and unsuspecting who felt any injury more keenly. Imagine having been imprisoned for years in Guantánamo, ridiculed, vilified, tortured, with no hope of release, and then suddenly to be set free and given entry to the homes of the very guards who'd sicced their Rottweilers on you while they'd jerked off and called you names. That, magnified many times, was Phil's devilish pleasure now, plus the sheer relief and release, sweeter than orgasm, of living again in the carefree flesh of his ten-year-old body, with no lingering smart of the lash, no parasites gnawing at his bowels, no talons ripping at his testicles when he collapsed onto the splintered toilet seat after another violent bout of diarrhea.

Thomas Mann was starting to get antsy. Much as he seemed to appreciate Phil's prepubescent ass in its snug uniform trousers, Mann's priority was still to continue with the seduction already at hand, in the accomplishment of which Phil's continued presence could only be an impediment. The old guy cleared his throat and swiveled his head as though to point the way to the door. Phil, lingering, asked like any other bellhop still waiting for his tip, "Will there be anything else, sir?"

Mann had already changed from his suitcoat to a smoking jacket before Phil had come into the room. Now he had to cross the carpet to where that coat was draped on the back of a chair, take his coin purse from the pocket, and winkle out a single bill from a small bundles of ones. Admittedly, this was 1939 — but still, what a piker!

"Why, thank you, sir," Phil said, slipping the bill into his trousers pocket. "Most kind. But let me —" Phil took up the coat from where Mann had thrown it in a heap atop the chair. "— hang this up for you, sir."

"There's no need for that, my boy," Mann protested in exasperation.

But his boy was not to be deterred, and he showed a similar valetish attentiveness to wiping the dry tabletop with his dry napkin.

At last, when he'd no idea how to buy more time, the drug took hold. The girl made a sound of stifled distress and pressed the champagne glass against her chest. "Excuse me, but I think I need to use your —" She managed to make two steps in the direction of the bathroom door and then collapsed onto the coffee table, overturning the ice bucket and the bottle of champagne, but preserving upright, miraculously, her own flute of champagne, still visibly fizzing.

"Oh dear! Oh, this can't be. Young man, help me get her onto the sofa."

The girl resisted their uncoordinated efforts, but feebly, and soon she was stretched out on her back, a cushion propping her head, the toque displaced at a comic angle.

"It can't be the little alcohol she's had. A single drink, and then the merest sip of champagne. Unless she'd had more before she appeared in the lobby. Oh dear, this is so unfortunate."

"Don't worry, sir," said Phil. "I'm sure she'll be better in a moment. Some ladies have a very small capacity. Not to worry, however. I can call the hotel's doctor, and he'll be here in a jiffy. If there is something *seriously* the matter, she can be taken to the infirmary."

"There is an infirmary here, in the Leamington?"

"It's a room that serves that purpose. She'll be more comfortable there. That is, if you would rather not tend to her yourself…?"

"Well, I'm concerned, of course. But she is not…traveling with me."

"She's not your responsibility you mean to say?"

Mann took a step backward and stared at Phil with the first glimmering of mistrust. "Perhaps we had better call the doctor."

"Just as you say, sir." Phil went to the bedside phone on the other side of the room and dialed Room 348.

Fletcher answered. "Yeah?"

"Dr. Nesbit?"

"Who!?" And then, "Oh yeah, this is Dr. Nesbit. And I'm speaking to Ish-ka-bibble?"

"Dr. Nesbit, we are having a small medical crisis in Room 334. Could you come here at once — and discreetly?"

"Sure thing. And, kid? Don't worry. I'll come on like Dr. Christian on that radio show just like we discussed."

"Thank you, Doctor." Phil returned the receiver to its cradle. "He'll be here shortly."

"Tell me," said Mann, switching to a sterner, lecturing tone, "who was it who ordered the champagne to be brought to my room?"

"I don't know, sir. It wasn't me who took the call. Some friend of yours, or the lady's, I suppose."

"And how did they pay for it?"

"I don't know, sir. You don't think there was something *wrong* with it, do you? You tasted it yourself." Phil picked up the glass that remained unspilled on the tabletop and sniffed at its still feebly bubbling contents. He placed the rim of the glass against his lips as though to sample it, but Mann intervened, taking the glass into his own hand.

"It wouldn't do, young man, to have you drinking alcohol in my room. I'm sure the champagne is quite all right. The bottle was sealed. You popped the cork yourself."

"That's true, sir," said Phil. And thought: and I poured it into the glass that I prepared myself. What the powder was, and how powerful its effects might prove, Phil hadn't bothered to ask those who'd provided it to him. He trusted the forces of hell to know their business in the matter of date-rape drugs and Mickey Finns. Hell's apothecaries had been perfecting their skills for centuries.

Again there was a knock at the door.

"That will be Dr. Nesbit," said Phil. He went to the door and admitted Fletcher, who was wearing a white dress shirt they'd purchased earlier around the corner from the hotel. Except for the Three Stooges haircut he seemed as plausible enough in his assumed identity as a doctor summoned after office hours, even down to the detail of the black bag he had with him. That bag with its contents of *materia medica* had been delivered to the Leamington and was awaiting them when they'd arrived, as was the parcel with Phil's bellhop uniform. They'd gone to the room reserved for them, a few doors down the corridor from this one, and there changed into the clothes they wore now. When one is dressed appropriately there's not a crime one can't commit.

"Please tell me how this came about," Dr. Nesbit asked with a deferential frown.

Mann offered what explanation he could. There was not much to tell, but while it was being told, Fletcher went through the motions of examining the girl's inert body, checking her pulse, tapping her chest, peering into her mouth. At last he stood up. "I think there is a simple remedy: a cold shower or sitz bath. We can do that here, or, if you prefer, I can take her to the infirmary."

"The infirmary, I think," Mann murmured with obvious relief. "I am anticipating other visitors in a little while."

"As you wish. I will phone as soon as the young lady is steady on her feet. Did she bring anything into the room with her?"

"Her handbag!" Phil scooped it up from where it peeked out from beside the couch and handed it to Fletcher. Together, with her limp arms draped over their shoulders, Phil and Fletcher dragged the drugged girl toward the door that Mann held open for them — and which he closed the moment they were in the corridor. It was a few moment's work to haul her into Room 348.

"You sure you want me to go ahead like we talked about?" Fletcher asked. Like the happier denizens of hell, Fletcher was wonderfully adaptable to any underhanded purpose and willing to follow any orders that accorded with his own appetites. He must have supposed that Phil was molded from the same compliant clay and following the orders of one or another of the malignant powers that be. Theirs not to reason why, theirs but to do and draw their pay.

"That's the plan," Phil agreed. "I'm sorry I can't stay and watch the fun. I'm sure that would add some spice for you, but I've got to get back to the old man before he thinks to call down to the desk. We've got to wrap this up and get out of here before the old boy's friends get back to the hotel."

"Whatever you say, kid. The rest of the job is all gravy — for me, anyhow."

"For me too, I expect," said Phil, giving a departing pinch to the cheek of the girl sprawled out on the bed. One of her shoes had gone missing, Cinderella-style, and the veil of her toque was tangled across her drooling mouth like the daintiest of gags.

On this visit back to his victim's hotel room Phil took along the homemade stun gun he'd assembled in his home workshop back in Oakland. It was a nuisance that he couldn't bring along a taser from hell's vast armory, but such were the laws of time travel that even Satan could not commit a physical anachronism. The *soul* of a malefactor might travel back in time — but he must use his own, or ancestral, flesh as his vehicle, and he could not return to the past with anomalous novelties, with iPods or Adidas sneakers or other loot from the future. He *could* avail himself of such insider information as racing results by way of funding his operations — and so Phil had, to the wonder and ravishment of Fletcher Nesbit.

Phil knocked one last time at the door of Room 334, and when Mann opened it, Phil gave it a good shove and then zapped[56] the old guy right where he figured his heart would be. He crumbled to the floor of the foyer with an almost inaudible *Ach!*

---

56 In 1967 Dick published a novel, *The Zap Gun* (Pyramid Books, 1967). It was one of his least considerable inventions, notable chiefly for the way it prefigures the murder of Thomas Mann.

Chapter Eighteen

THE WORLD IS ALWAYS coming to an end, especially for those with deep religious convictions. There is a whole branch of theology devoted to the subject — eschatology. Prophets have proposed various versions of that destined end, but a universal conflagration has been the consensus choice.

Valhalla, Carthage, Dresden, Hiroshima, Baghdad, and all the great cities still to be put to the torch as Western civilization winds down — it is a proud tradition, and an irresistible spectacle. In my grade school years I thrilled to see Victor Mature, as DeMille's Samson, tear down the temple of the Philistines, and while I came along too late myself to really believe in Godzilla, I could appreciate what he stood for: God as the Black Avenger, Destroyer of Worlds, Voice of the Whirlwind. The child who gleefully knocks down her own World Trade Center of building blocks will grow up to become the bland Omaha housewife engrossed in a bestseller detailing the systematic annihilation of the human race by God Almighty. It's not fiction for her, it's Holy Writ.

Did she but know it, I am her kind of god. *Schadenfreude* is my middle name. But I wasn't always the exterminator type. In my youth I was happy just to coast along in the great *Titanic* of western civilization, enjoying the continental cuisine and attending the concerts of the ship's orchestra. Bad things might happen, but always at a distance from the great ship of state. Americans especially were guaranteed safe passage. World War II had passed us by with an unscathed continent. I was twenty-six before I ever saw a bomb crater, and that had been left beside St. Paul's Cathedral in London as a kind of memorial, like the empty "footprints" proposed at the site of the rebuilt World Trade Center.

Since 9/11 and Bush's reelection and last Christmas's tsunami, things have begun to change and the sky to darken. In hindsight this new dispensation seems as inevitable as the fall of Troy once the Greeks' farewell present had been wheeled in through the city gate: *of course* western civilization is doomed; *of course* Germany and Italy and Spain will stop breeding their own offspring and hire Turks and Algerians to shovel their sidewalks and kill whoever may dis them; *of course* New York will become the new Rio de Janeiro, a haven for Eurotrash escaping from their own culture's collapse and eager to take lessons in rap and computer animation, the last two surviving arts; *of course* the snows will melt from Kilimanjaro, from the Alps and Andes and both the poles, and whales and penguins will become extinct, and so, in due course, will we.

Such is the handwriting on the wall, and we know whose finger scrawled it there. Even in Cassandra's day there must have been many Trojans who shared her prophetic intuitions and simply shrugged them off. The war had been going on so long, and the slaughter had been so great, and little was left worth having. Why make such a fuss? Why *not* go gentle into that good night, the way Virginia Woolf did when the Luftwaffe began laying waste to all of England? She simply slipped away, like Ophelia, and drowned herself in the nearest river. Some have written off her suicide as a last defense against incipient madness but who wants to stick around to watch the Nazis build new crematoria?

On the other hand, if there is no immediate necessity…if there are still groceries in the stores and fuel in the tank, if there are great old movies on DVD that one hasn't seen or has only a gossamer memory of, why then, why worry, what's the hurry, have another drink before you go.

Chapter Nineteen

VOLTAIRE'S FAMOUS EPIGRAM concerning the necessity of inventing gods when they don't exist is never more apposite than at times of danger and extremity, such as this. Not just the this of 1939, with the world on the brink of war and Thomas Mann lifeless in a bathtub at the Leamington Hotel, but also the this of 2005, with the world again on the brink of an even more calamitous and all-encompassing war, not to mention my own distress as I turn sixty-five in a few more days and must begin to pay some $800 a month for the prescription drugs that till now had cost me ten percent of that. *And*, most dire at all, the possibility that I may enjoy what Heine accounted the supreme happiness of never having drawn breath.

Well, let us deal first with 1939. There is really nothing I can do about Hitler's imminent invasion of Poland and all the horrors that will follow (though I must, in passing, recommend Isaac Bashevis Singer's *The Family Moskat*, a panorama of Jewish life in Warsaw in the years and moments before the Nazi juggernaut was set in motion). I can, however, in my role as a divinity in *this* sacred text, undo the mischief my nemesis has been up to and see that Philip K. Dick does not become America's own Quisling and the worst of all our bad presidents, as he has just prophesied to the dying Mann.

I have, as a kindness to my readers, omitted the rant he whispered into the unhearing ears of that great writer — a long false history of the coming victory of the Axis powers, somewhat as he and his wife Anne had mapped it out in *The Man in the High Castle* but modified with plot points lifted from Philip Roth's latest novel, *The Plot Against America*, which had recently come out in a pirated edition in hell to the delight of almost everyone there except Phil, who considered it a barefaced plagiarism.[57] Roth's success rankled in his shrunken soul, but it served his present purpose well. Its humdrum plausibility would be easy for Mann to believe and, so, to die despairing.

But World War II will *not* be revised and given a new unhappy ending, and Phil will remain the hack writer he always was, and die as Fate (*C'est moi!*) originally decreed — before his pulp fictions could make him a millionaire. Thomas Mann, on the other hand, will live to finish his Joseph tetralogy *and* his *Doctor Faustus* (which, by the by, was the spark that ignited my own *Camp Concentration*) and *Felix Krull*.

How can such things be, if Mann lies dead in the Leamington bathtub, electrocuted and then drowned for good measure, and my mother is raped and murdered before she could give birth to me? *That*, dear reader, is the great advantage of being God, as this final chapter in the marvelous saga of my birth will now make clear:

---

57 It's certainly not that, but it is, I think, a inferior work to the novel Dick wrote with Anne's and the *I Ching*'s assistance. What Roth's novel lacks is that quantum jump into a fictional realm truly Elsewhere. Roth's story is all too ploddingly probable.

Deus ex Machina

Red Disch had had one too many. Maybe more than one, in fact. Perhaps seven. He was tight, but not drunk, a fine distinction. Even so he decided that he had better ease back to a small glass of 3.2 beer before he hit the road again. He really should have found a bar closer to his hotel. In fact, he shouldn't have checked into the hotel at all. He'd had time to get home, maybe not by dinnertime but well before Jack Benny came on the air. And even if got home too late for Jack Benny he had a radio in the car now. He wouldn't have to miss a single joke.

The phone in the phone booth behind him rang, and the bartender, busy drawing beers from the tap, called out, "Hey, grab that for me, will you, Red?" Red shifted his seat from the barstool to the bench inside the booth, lifted the receiver, and then (unable to remember the name of the bar) said, "Uh-huh?"

He was more than tight, he was downright drunk, and that made him a pliant puppet for the god who now took hold of his strings. "Red," I said, in a fair imitation of my mother's voice. "Red, I'm in trouble."

"Helen? How in hell did you get my number here!"

"Never mind that. I'm in bad trouble. You got to come and get me. I'm downtown, at the Leamington Hotel."

"Christ's sake, Helen — what are you doing at the Leamington? It's almost eight o'clock. You should be home with Dad and Mom."

"Red, I can't talk about this right now. Okay? Just get here. I'm in Room 348. Hurry!"

Red was flabbergasted. Was Helen playing some kind of practical joke? Sometimes they would call up a new next-door neighbor (they moved around a lot, thanks to his being a traveling salesman) and tell them they had better cover their telephone with a damp towel because the phone company was going to be blowing the carbon out of the receiver. They'd give them a few minutes and then go over for a visit, and sure enough, the suckers would have taken the line. Helen always broke up. But this didn't sound like a joke. This sounded for real.

Red laid down three bucks on the damp counter, enough to cover his tab and still leave a tip, and then he went out to his Packard. It would take him an hour to get to downtown Minneapolis. A little longer because he'd have to stop and get gas. What could Helen possibly be up to at the Leamington? In one of the rooms upstairs! And how could she have known where to call him? Had she called every bar they'd ever gone to together? That would have taken a whole lot of dimes.

He was still mulling over the same unanswerable questions when he got to the Leamington forty minutes later. (He'd been doing 70 MPH most of the way; he hadn't thought the Packard had that much muscle, but it did.) He walked in like someone with his own room key, half under his own steam, half under mine, and headed for the broad red-carpeted staircase. The night clerk behind the desk didn't even look up.

Up the narrower staircase to the third floor, and down the corridor, past Room 334, and on to 348, where he paused to take a breath. Then, as he lifted his hand to knock, I took complete control — and lowered his hand.

Gods don't need keys to open doors.

Helen lay in the bed with Fletcher leaning over her, dazed and spent, with his pants about his ankles. Fletcher looked up at Red and smiled dopily. It was not the first time he'd been arrested in the commission of a crime, and he didn't panic. Indeed, he felt a small glow of accomplishment at having done the deed before he was undone himself.

Our eyes met, and Fletcher's closed as he slumped back nestling his head against Helen's breast.

Red smiled, in much the way God did when he rested on the seventh day, but for Red — for me — there was still work to be done. He left the victim and her rapist inert upon the blood-stained bedspread and exited the room to retrace his steps along the corridor to Room 334.

Again no key was needed.

Phil turned to face me when I appeared at the door of the bath-room. He seemed no more surprised than Fletcher had been, and no less self-satisfied. There was still a gleam of defiance in his myopic eyes but it was much diminished in intensity now that he knew his victim was dead.

"I hope you're the police," he said. "This man just tried to… to kiss me! And I don't know what else. But then he had a heart attack or something and fell into the bathtub. It was awful. I'm lucky to be alive."

"In fact, my boy, you're not alive. Or rather the spirit who has taken possession of your young flesh is not alive. And now he must leave that flesh and return —" I pointed my almighty finger at the boy and *wished* him very hard to his home in hell.

There was a distinct *pop*, like a light bulb the moment it shorts. The boy's face spasmed for a moment with demonic rage and then relaxed into its usual mask of spoiled sullen suspicion. Philip K. Dick, the paperback writer, had been snapped back to hell, like a bungee jumper bouncing home, and Phil Dick the ten-year-old wondered: "What the heck!"

"Run on down the hall to Room 348, my boy," I told him, "and wait outside the door." He did as he was told, leaving me alone with the corpse of Thomas Mann. I laid my right hand on the old man's forehead, with my thumb alongside the prominent vein that forked down from his hairline. "Arise," I bade him, "and be whole."

It was the first time that I had used my divine powers to bring someone back to life, and the sensation — for myself as much as for Mann — was extremely gratifying. He pushed himself into a sitting position, bracing his elbows against the sides of the tub for leverage. "God in Heaven! Whatever — ! I'm drenched. And who are you?"

"You had a fainting spell, sir, and the hotel doctor supposed it was a stroke. But you're quite all right, except for these wet clothes."

"This is outrageous."

"The hotel is profoundly sorry, sir. But you'll be happy to know that the young lady is also quite all right."

"The young lady? Oh. Oh yes. Her. Well, I'm glad to hear it."

"Perhaps you'd prefer to be left alone now, sir?"

"Indeed, yes. That would be best all round."

With a deferential nod, I left Mann extricating himself from his drenched smoking jacket and returned to Room 348. "You wait here," I told the chastened boy outside the door with a pat on his outsized head.

Inside Fletcher was where I'd left him, on the bed beside my mother, stroking her mussed hair. Her toque lay on the carpet, beside a single shoe. He looked up, with a wistful smile. "She's a looker, ain't she?"

I took pity on the poor man. Forgiving sinners is one of a god's prerogatives. Think of how Christ promised paradise to one of the thieves who'd been crucified at his side. Could I do less?

I placed my hand on Fletcher's brow, and winked. At once his warped soul was made straight. A new capacity for love and tenderness blossomed in the soil enriched by God's green thumb. "Go now, good fellow, and take the boy with you. Return to Oakland. And when you reach your destination, forget all these unfortunate events. Start life afresh, and make your children proud of you."

Fletcher kissed my hand reverently and departed.

And now it was Helen's turn, and Red's. As I'd resurrected Mann, so now I bade my mother return to life, and then, absconding, I released my father from his servitude to god's controlling power.

The happy couple regarded each other with wonder and amazement.

Such was the story of my birth.

Envoi

HAPPY BIRTHDAY TO ME! Here it is, February 2, 2005, and I have beaten my deadline by a couple of days and managed, retroactively, to arrange things so that I could be born. Or should I say be "born again"? In any case, the fact that you are reading this at all (whoever you may be) is proof that god exists (and I am he).

So much has happened already since Chapter 19 brought things to what I then supposed a happy ending. Now it looks more like a cliff-hanger, for though the book has won Charlie's approval (and received a final professional going-over from his red pencil) it was despised and rejected by my agent Glen Hartley, or rather, my *ex*-agent Glen Hartley, who, on the basis of having read the first half of the book, informed me that the manuscript was "a slap in the face" to the entire publishing industry. That did not seem to leave much room for further discussion, and so we have parted ways.

I would have been more devastated if I hadn't seen it coming for quite a while. Ten years ago I left my previous agent, Barnie Karpfinger, when Glen dangled before me as a *fait accompli* a contract to write a book about SF for the Free Press, then under the direction of his friend and my former student Adam Bellow. I took the bait, but before the delivery date for that book Bellow had been fired from Free Press, and the orphaned book barely made it through the production process. After that Glen never managed to sell any of my fiction, except three reprints to Vintage for piddling advances. Perhaps I should not have expected him to do any better, since he represents few living novelists. Newt Gingrich has been his most prominent client, and many of the other clients have been celebrity pundits of the far right. I thought I might dine at their table if I used a sufficiently long spoon, but I was wrong.

While I am not surprised, I am embittered, but even in that respect I have already had (unbeknownst to Glen) a sufficient revenge, for about a year ago, Glen and his partner/spouse, Lynne Chu, visited our New York apartment for the first time in four years (they live close by, but after a fire had wiped us out, Glen had been candidly squeamish about witnessing the resulting desolation), and on that visit he asked if he might buy the painting that then enjoyed pride of place behind my desk. I said yes, but named what I supposed would be a prohibitive price. He wrote out a check and left with the painting.

It is an acrylic on paper, 24 × 18 inches, under glass, with a black steel frame, and would seem, at a first glance to say, simply: EAT in large letters roughly slashed and slathered. I'd used the same basic design for three smaller pastels that had sold for $125 at a charity auction a few months earlier for *Parnassus* magazine. What neither Glen nor the winning bidder seemed to be aware of was that EAT was actually a close-up of a larger word, the initial D of which, and the terminal H, were indicated clearly enough if you gave the image much thought. I'm sure that even for those who are not consciously aware of the painting's little trick it must register at a subliminal level and exert an influence akin to that of the second-hand smoke in an English pub. It has been hanging, since Glen acquired it, in the main entrance space of his loft, but it may not remain there much longer, now that I am no longer a client. But that's all right. I'm sure it has already done its job.

ABOUT THE AUTHOR

THOMAS MICHAEL DISCH was born February 2, 1940, in Des Moines, Iowa. Enrolled in a succession of Catholic schools, he would develop, respectively, a love for classical music and opera, an opposition to the Catholic Church (seen regularly in his work), and a fascination for poetry and ballet. After moving to New York City in 1957, Thomas Disch enlisted in the army, just before his eighteenth birthday. He promptly went AWOL, was sent to a combination prison and mental hospital, and luckily was fairly promptly discharged. Returning to New York City, he began evening classes at NYU. In 1962, instead of cramming for midterms, he wrote the short story "The Double Timer," which was promptly sold for $112.50. Disch never returned to NYU, and instead took odd jobs as an insurance claims adjuster, a bank teller, a mortuary attendant, and a proofreader and copy editor to support his burgeoning writing habit.

Disch's voracity for writing has led him to create an astonishing range of publications. He has written science fiction (*Camp Concentration*, *334*), horror/gothics (*The Priest*), children's books (*The Brave Little Toaster*, *A Child's Garden of Grammar*), poetry (*Yes, Let's: New and Selected Poems*, *Dark Verses and Light*), book and theater reviews for *The Nation*, *Harper's*, the *Washington Post*, the *Los Angeles Times*, and *Entertainment Weekly*, poetry criticism (*The Castle of Indolence: On Poetry, Poets, and Poetasters*), media novelizations (*The Prisoner*), a computer game (*Amnesia*), and the libretto for an opera based on *Frankenstein*.

Amongst the awards Thomas Disch has received are the Braude, Campbell, Ditmar, O'Henry, British Science Fiction, Hugo, Locus, and Campbell awards, as well as the Pushcart Prize. He has been nominated for the National Book and the National Book Critic Circle awards. Disch has lived in Mexico, Spain, England, and Rome, but for the last twenty years he has lived mostly in New York City, where over the last few years he has been a radio pundit and theater critic, and is currently working on new fiction and poetry projects.